BILLIONAIRE'S CRUELTY

SUMMER COOPER

SUSU CHIN

Lovy Books Ltd
20-22 Wenlock Road
London N1 7GU

Created with Vellum
Cover by SC Creative

1

June

I didn't think I was capable of something like this. I stared at the printout of two business class tickets to Shanghai, one for me and the other one for Dave, Kai's personal bodyguard. All of this in the name of love. Just because the crush of my life finally kissed me then fucked me.

Our sex was ordinary. Not to say it wasn't great, it was just...ordinary.

Kai had a reputation in the sex department and what I had with him was clearly the more vanilla side of things. Nothing special. Just ordinary sex. No kink. No whips, no bondage, no blood. None of the stuff that he was known for.

But.

He was hungry for me. Like he had been waiting for me all his life and he wanted to treat me like the finest bone china. Unless it was all a clever illusion that he created to confuse me.

Naturally, I wanted more of him. In the meantime, I was scared the good times wouldn't last. It's like finally getting a piece of the best tiramisu in town, the one that's always sold out by the time you order it.

There was no denying it—I had to track him down. Rescue him if need be.

Nobody really knew what had happened to Kai. He was just in trouble. Again.

Although in comparison, his cousin Jenny seemed to be the one who was most likely to attract trouble than him. That woman didn't seem to be able to have a single peaceful day in her life. This whole situation was a rather eye-opening experience for me.

My big brother warned me about Kai's dark past. His family was on the rich list of China. People wanted things from them. Connections. Favors. The stubborn ones didn't play nice, causing mayhem until they got what they wanted from Kai or his family.

Kidnapping. Threatening. Blackmailing. Those were only a few of the things my brother was comfortable telling me about. There were more, he'd said, but he didn't want to overwhelm me with too much information.

As a doctor, I wouldn't wish harm on anyone. But when it comes to my loved ones? I would do that a thousand times over. I wanted those who hurt him or who brought him pain to pay for what they did.

I sat at the back of the getaway van feeling a little sick. A young man had booked two tickets for the next flight, and printed all the documents needed with a portable printer within ten minutes of us picking him up. One for Dave. One for me.

Kai had said many times that Dave was the best body-guard he ever had. Now, with a glimpse of how he oper-ated, with the help of his assistant, and his team, I had begun to understand what Kai meant.

The van finally stopped swaying. We parked outside of a no-parking zone at the airport. Without a word between us, we dashed out of the van and into the airport before the authorities had a chance to approach us.

Navigating around the airport seemed a little chal-lenging today. It appeared to be more chaotic than usual. Perhaps it was the car sickness caused by the fast and furious driving.

Or, as much as I wanted to deny it — the concussion from the car crash I'd caused on purpose to draw Kai out.

Dave handed me my passport as I checked the infor-mation board for our check-in desk.

"How the hell…"

"I stole it." He answered. His reply was straight and punchy. I opened my mouth to protest but nothing came out.

I flipped to the picture page, and it was indeed my passport.

I tried to remember where I'd left my passport, but I couldn't recall when I'd last seen it. When did Dave decide to take my passport? What else did he and his team go through at my home? Did they go through my personal belongings? My lingerie drawer?

My stomach lurched as I stared at Dave. Had he seen my toys?

We were actually a little early and that meant we could check in first and grab a few items from the duty free. Except we kept getting an error message at the check in machine. It wanted us to go straight to the desk.

I thought not having any baggage would save us time, but apparently not.

Dave picked up the phone his assistant handed him and spat something in Chinese.

Dave gripped my upper arm just under my armpit, dragging me off my feet. "We have to go." Dave hissed, his voice extremely low, but unmistakably clear.

"What's going on?" I knew he wasn't going to tell me anything, but I had to try.

Only one of my feet touched the ground, and my arm began to hurt.

"Ma'am, are you okay?" A lady in a security uniform asked. I realized how bad this looked.

I nodded.

"Do you need help?" The fat nosy woman raised her volume.

"I'm okay." I said, trying to sound as calm as I could.

"Put me down." I hissed at Dave, giving him a side glance letting him know that we were attracting unwanted attention.

"You don't look okay, girl. Do you know this man?" The woman wouldn't let it go. I hated how she felt like she had the right to police the airport. But then, I guess she did. The way Dave was manhandling me didn't help the situation.

"Yes, I, uh, I, um, injured my ankle earlier. He's just

helping me." I heard it as soon as I said it. It sounded like a lie.

I pretended to walk as funny as I could, limping here and there. But her droopy brown eyes narrowed and she saw right through me. "Your ankle looks okay to me."

Must she be so blunt?

"Go away." Dave growled, like a mad dog protecting his territory.

"Excuse me?"

Oh no. I could sense the coming confrontation before it even started—like it was my superpower. Maybe it was because I hated conflict so much.

The concerned expression on her face disappeared, replaced by the mean, nasty one that all school principals seemed to possess. She planted her fists on her waist sending a nervous shiver down my back.

This thing with this nosy woman had gone on for far too long.

Whatever matter that was on Dave's mind must have been important and urgent. And I had underestimated how much Kai's disappearance would affect Dave.

"Excuse my *friend*... he didn't mean it." I said slowly, with my calm doctor voice.

"I'm going to call the police." She declared at the top of her lungs, causing passers-by to stop and stare.

"No, no need to call the police." I yanked Dave's hand off of me.

"Ma'am, you're in danger. I can tell."

"No, no, no. I'm not in danger." I shook my head and chuckled lightly as I tried to explain. Dave's assistant was poking furiously on his phone — he better be calling back up right about now.

"You are if you don't let us go now."

A statement.

A dare.

This was bad news.

"Shut. Up." I grumbled under my breath.

I would come up with creative and unpleasant names to call him, if I wasn't so scared of confrontation, conflict, and making a scene.

"Are you threatening me?" The woman asked then pointed at Dave's assistant then back at him. "You. Are you with him? What are you doing on your phone?"

"Of course not." I said, interrupting what looked like it was going to be the next viral video in the making. "He's not. They are not. I don't know them."

Words tumbled out of my mouth, no longer making sense.

Dave's hand was back on me, this time on my shoulder, urging me away from the situation.

Whether he knew it or not, I wanted to get out of here as much as him.

"Call for backup." The woman yelled at her walking talkie next to her shoulder.

"Don't call for backup." What backup? Who was this woman other than a rent-a-cop? Who else was with her?

"We go now." Dave's assistant moved swiftly next to me and put his hand on my other shoulder. Any minute now, I would have no say in where I was going.

"Ma'am, I work for the airport security. You're safe with me."

My stomach twisted, like it was reacting to a bad lunch.

"We *really* have to go." Dave's words hung in the air, but they did nothing to change the fact that we were still trapped here.

Though I knew it was coming, a scream still escaped my mouth as two pairs of hands hoisted me off the floor.

"Where the fuck do you think you're going?" Needless to say, she was angry now. A pair of cuffs appeared from her back.

"No." Dave's roar was so loud. My head snapped to my shoulder, instinctively shielding my ear.

"Sorry, assholes, you're not going anywhere."

One second, we were on our feet, then all three of us hit the floor hard. No question about it: we'd been tackled.

"Mack got out." Dave half-grunted, half-whispered in my ear. "You need to run."

How was that possible? Was that why Dave was acting so strange?

I had so many questions, but now wasn't the time to ask them—not while we were still pressed to the ground, trapped inside the cave of attackers.

When I was finally pulled back to my feet, I saw that Dave and his man were hand cuffed. Each of them was retrained by two large men wearing the same uniform as the mean bitch who had confronted us. Dave shook his head, mouthing a few words at me—I couldn't make them out—but I knew it could only mean one thing.

Feeling the cold touch of metal against my wrist, I panicked. Shoving the guy next to me, I ran as fast as I could without looking back. They were after me—I knew that much. If they were just concerned about of a woman possibly being abused, why would they bother cuffing me? Who cuffs the victim?

Outside, I spotted a car that had just dropped off a passenger and jumped in without hesitation. "Go, go, go!"

"Get the fuck out!" the driver barked in his thick accent.

"Twenty thousand dollars if you drive me to Myrtle Beach!" The words blurted out of my mouth before I had a chance to stop them. I couldn't believe how much I sounded like my mother—trying to solve my problems by throwing money at them.

"Thirty."

Seriously? Did he have no morals? Who haggles with a distressed woman?

"Fine," I wasn't going to win this haggling game, and he knew it.

"Fifty."

What a greedy piece of shit!

"Go, go, go!" I screamed as I spotted the men approaching the car.

He grunted something in a foreign language. Finally, he hit the gas, peeling away from the curb.

I hadn't exactly thought this through. To be fair, I wasn't given much time. And now, I was stuck in a near ten-hour drive with a stranger—one who had possibly just saved my life for a reward of fifty thousand dollars.

"So... are you, like, an Uber driver or something?"

I figured I might as well make conversation. Besides, if

he turned out to be some kind of serial killer, I'd at least die knowing how that happened.

"You can say that." He said, his voice rough and disinterested. His accent was thick—Indian, maybe—but there was more to it.

"What's your name?" I asked, looking for a clue.

"Listen miss, I'm not telling you my name. If you really need one, just call me Raj."

"Raj? Really?" I scoffed. "You don't look like an Indian dude."

"Yes, but I sound like one, don't I?"

He was as white as my dad—and as white as any white Americans that I'd ever met. "Not really. Were you born here?"

A deep, drawn-out sigh escaped him. "Alright, since we've got a long drive ahead of us, I'll tell you. But you'll have to tell me why you're running."

"Deal."

Up until now, he hadn't asked me how I planned to pay him. He must've noticed I didn't have anything on me. Still, I couldn't help but appreciate his trust—or maybe he wasn't planning to take me to Myrtle Beach at all. I shook the thought away and focused on our conversation.

"I was adopted," he said, as if that explained everything. "My parents were illegal immigrants from, uh, Asia. The poor couple couldn't have kids. Prayed for a child night and day. Then, *viola*, one evening, they found me in a dumpster behind their house."

"Wow. Really?" My voice dripped with skepticism.

"Sounds ridiculous, huh? It's true."

"Why didn't they turn you into the authorities?" I asked, struggling to believe a story like this could still exist in this day and age.

Raj let out a short laugh.

"Wow, really?" he said, mockingly. "Now who's the white dude, here? My parents are great. They raised me up like their own. And trust me—going through the system wouldn't have given me a better life."

He shifted his grip on the steering wheel and cast me a sideway glance. "Now your turn. Why are you running? Who were those people at the airport?"

I stared out the window, trying to organize my thoughts. Where did I even begin—and how much should I tell Raj?

"My abusive husband—"

"Cut the crap." Raj snapped. "And what's your name, by the way? I told you mine."

"June." I said, deciding against making one up. I couldn't bring myself to care.

"Alright, June—just tell me the truth."

So, I did.

I told Raj about Mack—a member of a Hong Kong triad—how he tried to hurt me but was arrested, only to be released soon after for no apparent reason. How he was later kidnapped by my rich friend's security team, but he somehow escaped. And now, he was after me.

"That's why I'm running. My friend's security team was helping me at the airport, but we got attacked. I got away and somehow ended up in your car."

I knew that we were in a Toyota, but I couldn't tell the

model. Probably one of those hybrids everybody seemed to love.

"Interesting. You know they're not airport security, right?"

"What?"

"The people chasing you—they're not airport sec–"

"I heard you," I interrupted. "I mean, how do you know?"

He shrugged. "I just know. Their uniforms look wrong."

He went on and explained—something about the color being off, the stitching, the badges in the wrong places. I nodded along, but my mind drifted. If that woman at airport wasn't actually airport security... then who the hell was she? And was she after me or Dave?

"You okay?" His voice softened, and for the first time, he actually sounded concerned.

"I'm fine, thanks. Where are we, anyway?"

We'd been on the road for two hours, but nothing outside looked familiar.

"Took a detour. We'll stop in ten. I know a place." His tone was casual. A little too casual. The unfamiliar roads outside the windows sent bad thoughts through my mind and a chill down my spine. Maybe I'd listened to too many true-crime podcasts, but something about this felt... off.

Ten minutes later, we pulled into a diner in the middle of nowhere. Wendy's Home Cooking. I made a mental note. Easy enough to remember—since I had a friend called Wendy.

"I'm hungry. Are you hungry? Do you need something to eat?" he asked as he killed the engine.

"I don't have any money on me." I admitted, "but I swear—you'll get paid when we get to Myrtle Beach. My brother will cover it, I promise."

"Relax. I know the owner of this place. Order whatever you want—I'll be there in a sec."

He got out of the car, and I followed. He popped open the trunk and pulled out a screwdriver.

"What are you doing?"

"Changing the plates. We're on the run, right? Can't have anyone tracking us halfway to Myrtle Beach."

I stood there, watching him swap the plates like it was the most normal thing in the world.

"Do you do this all the time?" I asked. "How many other plates do you have back there? Who are you really?"

He chuckled under his breath. "Calm down, princess."

Princess.

My stomach dropped. Was it just a fluke? Or did he know who I really was?

I bent down, snatching a crowbar from the trunk, and swung it behind my head.

"Who the fuck are you?"

He raised his hands, palms out. "Easy. Let's go inside —I'll explain, okay?"

"No. You're going to explain right now, and don't think I'm afraid of a little blood."

That was a lie. I hated blood—hated the sight, the smell, everything about it. But I wasn't about to let him know that. And I'd discovered it too late to back out of medical school.

His face softened. "I'm a friend. Okay? That really rich friend of yours—she hired me to follow you."

"Kai? You know where he is?"

"Huh? No, it's a woman—Rocks, I think."

Roxie. That was Chloe's stripper name. She'd gone back to being Chloe, but I guess she still used the old name when it suited her.

"Prove it." It didn't hurt to be a little careful at this point. "Prove to me that you know her."

"We need to go in the diner. Come on. Her real name is Chloe. She's married to Lincoln. "

"I'm not convinced." I raised the crowbar higher.

"Wait, wait!" He raised his hands higher in response to my movement, panic flashing across his face. "She said if you didn't believe me, to say something about that show you used to watch. Uh... *Dirty Little Liar!*"

Pretty Little Liars.

"Close enough," I muttered.

I dropped the crowbar, relieved that he wasn't a serial killer, though a little disappointed that he had no connection to Kai.

Inside Wendy's, the cashier took our orders. When she returned, she handed me a brown paper bag. Inside I saw some cash, a change of clothes, and an old-fashioned flip phone.

"Please, close your mouth, people will stare," Raj commented, smirking. "You can trust us, here. We'll eat something now, grab a few things for the road, and you should change before we head out."

The remaining journey to Myrtle Beach was surprisingly pleasant. I learned that Raj was my friend Wendy's cousin, and when he wasn't following runaway women, he helped his parents run a laundromat in New York. He'd been tailing me ever since Chloe found out about Mack from Wendy—because, apparently, Wendy couldn't keep a secret from Chloe.

Knowing I'd been followed by both Kai's and Chloe's people over the last few days was weird. My privacy had been violated from every angle. But without them, I'd probably be knee-deep in a thousand different kinds of trouble.

2

Kai

Whoever did this to us will pay.

This had to be an inside job.

I'd doubled the security for Jenny, terrified her husband might find her. The extra team that I hired came with glowing reviews and high-level recommendations—from politicians, mayors, senators, and even unnamed foreign dignitaries. When they dropped their most impressive reference—a former President of the United States—they were outraged to discover I had no clue which one they were talking about. Well, sue me for not memorizing every single U.S. President.

For all I knew, the entire thing could've been fake. These days, it wasn't hard to fabricate anything. There were professionals who wrote glowing reviews in exchange for cash—and others who specialized in writing scathing ones to ruin their competitors. Trust no one—especially not on the Internet.

Even people could be fake.

Asian social media had been buzzing with rumors that Catherine, Princess of Wales was dead and had been quietly replaced by a doppelganger. Something about the prince's obsession with a new mistress and his eagerness to be rid of his wife. Could it be true? Who knows. But if they could fake a royal, they could fake anything.

"Can I get you any tea or coffee?" Jessica, the flight attendant, leaned in closer to my seat, batting her thick black lashes. Fake. Nobody on the planet came with eyelashes as thick as rabbit fur. Her platinum blond hair, with visible tracks, was also fake. I wondered what else about her wasn't real.

"Just water," I answered.

Jessica was trying to be helpful—trying to make the flight easier and distract me from the mess I was in. She'd said as much the second I stepped on the plane. I wouldn't say we had history, but we'd definitely had our share of good times. That was over now. Right now, I needed to focus.

Because the only woman I wanted was stuck in a hospital.

Dr. June Bennet—the world's greatest fertility doctor, according to every magazines and medical journal that mattered. She was busy fixing someone's life, making their dreams of having a family come true, maybe even saving their marriage. Meanwhile, I was here—failing to protect that people I cared about.

When she finished her procedure, she'd find the note I left on the desk. A promise—I'll be back soon.

I should've texted her. Something simple. "I'm okay.

Don't worry." But every time I tried, my finger froze. She'd ask questions that I didn't want to answer. I couldn't lie to her. And call me a coward, but I didn't want her to worry—not about me, not about Jenny, not about Lucy.

"Sir, do you want the whole team at the airport when we land?" Clare's voice cut through my thoughts, softer than her usual tone. She'd been apologizing repeatedly since Jenny and Lucy were taken. If I hadn't told her to shut up, she would probably still be apologizing. I'd deal with her later—right now, I needed her focused. I'd already left Dave behind to keep watch over June.

"I don't want the whole team. Just the Range Rover."

"Are you sure?" As always, she questioned my orders.

"Yes."

A beat of silence. Then, carefully, she asked her next question. "What is your plan? If I may ask."

I tilted my cream leather recliner back, my gaze fixed on my own hand. I couldn't bear to look at her, couldn't stand to.

"What could you possibly do with that information, huh?" My voice came out low, cold—venom laced through every word.

I knew she couldn't have predicted what happened. No one could have. Jenny and Lucy had been taken in broad daylight—right outside one of the most high-profile hair salons in New York. A place crawling with the rich and famous and their bodyguards and security. We all thought it was safe.

The Japanese owners were probably still pissing themselves after my phone call—after I swore to sue their asses for losing my pregnant cousin and her best friend, two heirs to the most powerful billionaire families in China.

I'd been too easy with Clare. Too relaxed. Her bubbly, outspoken personality—completely wrong for a bodyguard—had made Dave's life easier. And after everything he'd done, everything he'd sacrificed to keep me safe, I wanted him to have a break before he finally retired.

Look where that got us.

There was no way Clare didn't know I was still angry —at her, at the whole damn thing. And I wanted to keep it that way. It was the only time I'd seen her this professional, this polite, and I had to admit—I kind of enjoyed it.

For once, there was no smart comeback. She just nodded and walked away, leaving me at peace with my own thoughts.

The truth? I had no plans.

I should have left for Shanghai the moment I heard about Jenny's abduction.

Instead, I wasted time. Precious time.

I stayed in New York, getting my affairs in order— splitting my team and assigning each member to handle different tasks. Loose ends that didn't matter as much as Jenny's safety. I told myself it was necessary, but deep down, I knew the truth—I was stalling. And worse, when I should've been on a flight halfway across the world, I found myself standing in front of Mack.

I didn't even know what drove me there. Fear? Maybe. Or the gnawing need to confirm he wasn't involved. I could have sent Dave to do the dirty work, but I needed to see Mack's face when I asked the question.

Did you take her?

The bastard smiled like I was some fool playing a losing game.

"I don't know your cousin," he said, leaning back against the cold concrete wall. His face bruised, swollen —still held that smugness I couldn't stand.

I wanted to believe him. I did. Something about the way he said it—too calm, too casual—itched at the back of my skull. I pressed harder. Asked again. Then he dropped the bomb. "You're asking the wrong questions. The real mystery is June."

My heart slammed against my ribs.

"What the hell are you talking about?"

He licked the blood from his lip, eyes gleaming like he knew he'd hooked me. "She's been keeping secrets from you. Big ones."

I lost it. My fist connected with his face before I even realized I'd moved. One punch. Then another. Harder. And harder. I hit him until my knuckles split, blood dripping warm and slick between my fingers. Still, he laughed —low, hoarse, defiant.

Secrets. What the hell was he talking about?

For all I knew, he was just saying that to mess with me.

I'd had enough of incompetent, annoying people for the day. Anyone who dared talk to me during this flight would be testing both my patience and my temper. I shut my eyes and leaned back. Pretending to sleep had always been the easiest way to get people to leave me the hell alone.

I knew the Chens had been looking for Jenny—I just didn't think they'd bother searching New York. Last I heard, they were chasing ghosts across Europe. I'd made sure of that. My guys planted a dozen false leads in Paris —restaurant reservations, fake addresses, even parcels addressed to Jenny. It was hilarious imagining Chen's men combing through boutique hotels, only to find boxes of overpriced shoes bought with the credit card he'd given her.

That little trick should've kept them chasing their tails for a while. Someone must have tipped them off, there was no way in hell Chen figured it out on his own.

I didn't want to leave New York. Not when Mark—or Mack, or whatever the hell his name really was—still locked up in a garage on the outskirts of the city.

I didn't know the full story between him and June. I was waiting for her to tell me when she was ready. But I knew one thing—he wasn't afraid to hurt her. When the police released him without pressing charges, it was clear he had friends in high places. I wasn't about to sit back and wait for him to try again. So, I took matters into my own hands.

I had him snatched off the streets before he could get anywhere near her.

My only concern was how long it would take before his powerful friends came looking for him. It wouldn't take much to connect him to June—and from there, to me. When that time came, I could call in my own powerful friends, including June's brothers. But until I knew exactly who I was up against, I wasn't making any moves.

For now, I trusted Dave to keep her safe. He'd spent most of his life protecting me—valuing my safety above his own. There was no one better.

The Shanghai skyline greeted us with a gorgeous golden sunset as we touched down.

On the tarmac, two black vehicles idled, waiting for us. Clare had ignored my instructions and called in a second car. I let it slide. She knew I was too tired to care. And she was right—having backup was the smart move.

Jessica and the new blond stewardess bowed as I stepped off the plane. Without a second glance, I headed straight for the Range Rover, Clare trailing behind me. I raised a hand, gesturing for her and the rest of the team —two others—to take the second car.

"*Ni hao,* boss." Mario greeted excitedly, his jaw grinding on a piece of gum.

The cocky troublemaker had been working for me for nearly ten years. His job? Causing problems for anyone who crossed me. Today, he wore a black vest that did nothing to hide the ink on his arms—a bold symbol of his clan, or whatever they called the mafia in New York. The tattoos, combined with his unruly energy, made him look even more dangerous than he already was.

He pulled open the back door for me.

I gave him a brief nod as I slid inside, letting him shut the door behind me. Normally, I'd return his greeting with a sarcastic "*Buongiorno,*" mimicking a bad Mario impression. But not today.

"To Chen's residence." I ordered as he settled into the driver's seat.

A slow, wicked grin spread across his face. "Love the smell of trouble."

"Did you find out anything?" I asked, cutting straight to business.

Mario snorted. "Of course. I ain't lazy, and I don't take your salary for granted."

With my usual private investigator coming up short, I'd sent Mario to dig deeper. I wanted anything, *everything* on Mack. But Jenny's disappearance had not come first.

"I've also got some dirt on Chen you might find interesting."

"Let's hear it."

"Chen's chick—Anna Wang? Turns out she's not even Chinese." Mario said, diving straight into the gossip. Apparently, he'd decided that was what I wanted to hear about first.

I remembered Anna—young, wild, and a known party animal. Early twenties, at most. Her Mandarin was so flawless that no one would've ever doubted she wasn't born and raised in China.

"American?" I guessed.

"No, Australian. Like born and bred." Mario added, cracking his gum. "She probably thought life would be easy—snag a sugar daddy like Chen and live the dream. But..."

He let out a low whistle. "God knows what that sick bastard made her do. Whatever it was, things went dark.

Ugly. Her parents found out, and now they want to sue his ass."

"What kind of 'bad shape' are we talking about?" I pressed, though I already had a sinking feeling in my gut.

"Kinky shit, boss." Mario's voice dipped lower, the usual teasing edge replaced by something darker. "My nurse friend said Anna was bruised... in places. And they found Barbie dolls up her pussy."

I turned my head slowly toward him. "Did you say... Barbie? Children dolls?"

"Yeah, three of 'em, boss. Apparently, there were five, but she managed to get two out herself. The other three? Stuck. She ended up in the hospital with a nasty infection and a fever."

Jesus Christ. Even for Chen, this was twisted. But this wasn't just disturbing–it was useful. Another victim meant a pattern. A potential case against him. And if I could find Anna, I might have the leverage I needed to keep Jenny safe.

"Where is Anna now?"

Mario shrugged, popping his gum. "No one's seen her since she got discharged. Either she skipped town... or Chen got to her first."

I didn't like either possibility. If Anna was smart, she'd be hiding. But Chen had already cleaned up his mess, she might not be alive to testify. Either way, tracking her down became another item on my ever-growing to-do list.

I shifted the direction of the conversation. "And the other thing I asked you to do?"

Mario straightened up, his usual easygoing manner turning serious. "Mack Ander."

"Yes. What did you find out?"

He cleared his throat. "He's a drug dealer, boss. Serious drug dealer."

That didn't surprise me. I'd already suspected Mack wasn't clean—but Mario's tone told me there was more to the story.

"So?"

"Not just local. Hong Kong, Taiwan and parts in China. That means he's in bed with some really powerful triads."

I shook my head, unimpressed. "What's the big deal? You know people who push product right? Hell, I've seen you dabble."

Mario snorted. "Yeah, but that's an occasional treat. This guy? He's bad news. And working across multiple territories? That's a death wish."

That got my attention. "What do you mean?"

"He's working for everyone—double-crossing the biggest players in the game. And when they find out? They won't be happy." He let out a long breath. "You know that code, right? You pick a side and stick to it until you're six feet under. This guy broke every rule."

"So, every triad wants him dead?"

"Pretty much."

I leaned back, digesting the information. It made sense—sort of. Mack's life being in danger explained why he fled to the United States. But there was a missing piece.

"If he's that screwed, how the hell did he get out of the jail there?"

"I'll see what I can find out."

What I really wanted to know was—how did June know Mack?

Maybe they crossed paths during one of her business trips.

Or maybe there was something darker. Was it possible she had a drug problem no one knew about? But even if she had bought drugs from Mack before, it didn't explain why he would follow her or attack her like that.

I pushed the thought aside as Chen's property came into view.

Jenny and Chen owned multiple properties in Shanghai, but I knew he wouldn't risk taking her to one of their sleek penthouses downtown—that would draw too much attention. No, he'd take her somewhere private. Somewhere isolated.

The mansion on the outskirts of Shanghai.

It was a sprawling estate, surrounded by acres of land and high walls. Out here, neighbors weren't just distant—they were indifferent. Whatever happened behind those gates would stay hidden. If Chen wanted to hurt her, no one would hear a thing.

As we rolled up to the entrance, there was no warm welcome. No staff waiting by the gate. They weren't expecting us. They sure as hell didn't want us there.

I tried the polite approach first, buzzing the intercom.

A bored voice crackled through the speaker. "No one's home."

Frankly, I didn't buy it.

"Boss, what's the play?" Mario's voice cut through the tense silence. His eyes gleamed with anticipation—finally, some action.

He'd come to Shanghai chasing a fantasy—the city ruled by triads and gangsters, like in the old movies. But modern Shanghai wasn't the blood-soaked battleground he'd imagined. Truth was, he would've found more action if he'd stayed in New York. Still, something about the city —maybe the culture, maybe the formidable Shanghai women—had kept him here.

And now, after years of waiting, he had a chance to cause the kind of chaos he craved.

I met his gaze, feeling an eerie sense of calm. Under normal circumstances, the word kidnapping alone would've sent my pulse racing. But right now? I felt in control.

"What do you have in mind?" I asked, though I already knew the answer.

Mario grinned, his teeth flashing like a wolf about to tear into prey.

"Run down the gate..." He trailed off with a low, psychotic laugh, and I had no doubt he had far more violent ideas he wasn't voicing.

I nodded. "That's our only option."

"Do it," I ordered.

Mario's smile stretched wider as he shifted gears. "With pleasure, boss."

There was no point wasting time. Whoever was inside wasn't going to let us in. And that's why I'd told Clare to bring the Range Rover. It wasn't just any luxury SUV.

Mario had personally modified the car, reinforcing it with custom brackets designed to absorb heavy impacts. Just in case things ever got messy, he padded the car with bulletproof glass and swapped out the engine for one meant for a monster truck. Power was never a problem.

"Breaking and entering—here I come."

"That's illegal here." I teased, though I had no plans to stop him from destroying Chen's property.

Mario let out a dry chuckle. "Yeah, yeah. So is kidnapping a woman."

He flexed his fists like it might somehow help with ramming through a steel gate. With a quick reverse, he angled the car just right.

"You're not wrong."

Without another word, he slammed his foot on the gas.

The Range Rover shot forward, colliding with the gate in a thunderous crash.

"You know boss," he said almost too casually, "the car is less likely to stall if you hit it from the side. Plus, we're safer that way."

I raised an eyebrow. "Great tips—I see you've done this before."

The jolt sent a thrill coursing through me. But when the gate still stood, I couldn't help adding, "but the gate's still standing."

Mario grinned, undeterred. "One or two more hits. Promise."

He eased the car back, revving the engine like a madman who lived for destruction. The deeper the growl, the more the tension in my chest built. For a moment, I imagined Chen's face when we rolled up uninvited—smashing down his precious gate like it was nothing.

Mario gunned it again.

This time, the gate buckled under the impact, twisting and groaning before it finally gave way.

"Told ya," he said, triumphant, as he accelerated up the driveway.

The road was lined with towering, ancient trees—deliberately planted to shield the mansion from prying eyes. Not that it mattered now. As we drove further in, I spotted the security guards ahead. Their wide-eyed expressions? Pure gold.

"I saw my pop do this once," Mario mused, like we were taking a Sunday drive. "Didn't even scratch the car. But the poor sucker he hit? Dead on the spot."

His words hung in the air, dark and casual.

"What happened to your dad?" I asked, genuinely curious. Mario rarely talked about him—although I knew his father was part of an old and powerful Mafia family.

He shrugged. "Nothing."

"Nothing? Your dad killed someone and nothing happened?" I tried to sound neutral. But his overly relaxed manner had me on edge.

"Yeah, it was a hit–and–run. Late at night. No witnesses." Another shrug, like it was really no big deal.

"Interesting."

"Haven't you seen any true crime shows?" Mario's voice took on a singsong lilt, as if he was reciting a twisted nursery rhyme. "People get away with murders. Lots and lots of people. Lots and lots of people…"

His laughter echoed through the cabin, low and unsettling.

And as we drew closer to the mansion's entrance, I had the distinct feeling that things were about to get much darker.

3

June

Fifteen hours of driving later Raj and I arrived at Myrtle Beach just after midnight. The journey had been quiet and uneventful after we set off from Wendy's, which suited me just fine. Raj and I had exchanged a few casual conversations along the way, but nothing too personal. That was how I preferred it.

I'd spoken to Chloe on the burner phone the waitress left for me in the little brown bag. Raj had given her a vague update about my situation, but she was relieved when I finally called. When I asked Chloe to get $50,000 in cash ready for Raj, she seemed a little reluctant. But I wouldn't take no for an answer. Regardless of who Raj was working for, I intended to keep my promise.

When Raj dropped me off at Lincoln and Chloe's beach house, Chloe handed him a brown paper bag—which I could only assume contained the money. As much as I wanted to invite him to stay, I held back. It wasn't my house, and I had no right to offer him shelter.

Chloe gave me a quick hug and led me through the massive hallway into their open kitchen. I sank silently onto a stool at the kitchen island, watching as she busied herself with quiet efficiency. The house was as sleek and elegant as I remembered—high ceilings, marble counter-tops, and a faint scent of the ocean wafting in through the open balcony doors.

A few moments later, she placed a cup of chamomile tea in front of me. Only then did I realize what she was doing—trying to calm me down. My mind was too rest-less for that. "I think I need something stronger. Can I have a coffee?"

Chloe frowned lightly but obliged. "Okay."

She plugged in the coffee machine, filled it with decaf, and pressed the start button, then immediately removed the plug from the wall once the coffee was done. I almost protested. Decaf wouldn't clear the fog clouding my thoughts. But I stayed quiet, observing the delicate way she handled the machine.

After all these years, Chloe still hadn't fully got over her fear of fire. Who could blame her? If I had lived through two major fires, I'd be cautious too.

"I'm so glad you're okay." Chloe said softly, sliding the mug across the counter to me.

"Thanks. I don't know how to thank you."

"I'm sorry I didn't tell you I had someone watching over you," she admitted, shifting her weight from one foot to the other. "But I knew—"

"You knew I'd hate it if I found out."

"Yeah." She nodded. "Lincoln wanted to send one of his guys, but I thought it would be better coming from me. Don't you think?"

I forced out a small chuckle. "You're right. The idea of my big brother knowing everything I do would drive me insane."

Chloe adjusted the champagne-colored nightgown she wore, pulling the silky robe tighter around her waist. Her figure was as stunning as ever, even after her pregnancy.

"But if it weren't for Wendy's cousin, I don't know where I'd be right now."

"Don't be silly. That's why Raj was the perfect person for the job. He isn't restricted by any code or rules like a regular bodyguard. He's just a friend, looking out for another friend."

"How did you know I'd run out of the airport?" I asked. The thought had been nagging me since I got in Raj's car. "Did you put a tracker on me or something?"

"I didn't," she laughed lightly. "Believe it or not, we didn't think you would have any trouble at the airport. It was luck that Raj wanted to wait, just in case."

"So, Raj... Is that his real name?" I tilted my head, curious.

"Yes, why?"

"I thought it was fake." The decaf was surprisingly effective. My mind felt sharper.

Chloe grinned. "Odd, right? His adoptive parents gave him that name. He has a birth name, but he doesn't use it."

"So, no dumpster story?" I joked, remembering the tale Raj had spun.

"Dumpster?" Chloe's confused expression told me that part of his story had been pure fiction.

"Never mind. Enough about Raj. Is Lincoln awake? I need to talk to him."

"June, you look exhausted. You should rest first."

"No, I need to talk to my brother," I insisted.

Chloe hesitated, concern clouding her face. "Are you sure? Whatever you need, we can handle it tomorrow."

"I won't be able to sleep if I don't talk to him," I said, my voice rising. "Lincoln! Link!"

"Shhh! The kids are asleep." Chloe reached across the island, brushing her manicured fingers against my cheek to quiet me.

"Get Link," I whispered.

"Fine. Just wait here."

I could have stormed upstairs and found him myself, but the house was enormous. And knowing their... *intimate* hobbies, the last thing I wanted was to stumble upon my brother in a compromising situation. Naked. Tied up. Ew.

Two minutes later, Lincoln appeared, dressed in grey-and-white striped pajamas. Seeing him like that brought back memories of childhood sleepovers when Chloe used to stay with us. Back then, he was the bossy older brother who always knew best—some things never changed.

"Juney," he said, pulling me into a hug. His arms wrapped around me tightly, the warmth of his embrace easing some of the tension coiled inside me. "You okay? I was worried sick."

"I'm fine. See? Still in one piece." I wiggled my fingers for emphasis, trying to lighten the mood. But my voice cracked lightly, betraying how far from fine I really felt.

Lincoln leaned back, scanning my face with that sharp, assessing gaze he reserved for boardrooms and family emergencies. "Why were you at the airport?"

"I was planning to go to Shanghai," I admitted. My heart pounded as I rushed into the next part. "And that's why I need to ask—can I borrow your plane?"

His expression didn't change. Damn, he had a good poker face. Not even a flicker of surprise.

"You want to borrow my plane?"

"I can't fly it myself, obviously. I mean, I need a private plane to China. Your pilot. The whole package."

A faint noise drifted down from upstairs—a thump, followed by the sound of quick, light footsteps. Lincoln's head tilted slightly, his brow furrowing.

"Hang on," he murmured stepping past me.

"They should be asleep," Lincoln muttered under his breath, but there was no real annoyance in his voice— just the kind of exasperation only a parent could feel. He started up the stairs but paused midway, turning back down. "Hold that thought. I need to make sure no one's trying to break my house rules."

I couldn't help but smile as he disappeared.

When he returned, he shook his head with a mixture of fondness and frustration. "They're conspiring against me. Apparently, bedtime is just a suggestion."

I laughed softly, feeling strange seeing this side of my

brother for the first time. "Well, you always did have a problem with authority."

He snorted.

"Yeah, and now I'm the authority no one listens to." His smile faded. "About the private jet—yes."

"Thank you" I jumped up and wrapped my arms around him, kissing his cheek.

"Don't thank me yet," he warned, pushing me away. "You need to answer all my questions first. No answers, no deal."

I groaned. "Why can't you just do me a favor without making it complicated?"

"Because I care about you," he said, brushing his hand along my upper arm.

"Fine. What do you need to know?"

I told him everything about wrecking my Tesla, luring Dave out of hiding, the fake airport security, and Mack. I held nothing back.

"You were lucky Raj was there," Lincoln said after a pause.

"You could say that. I owe all of you—Raj, Chloe and you. Happy now?"

My big brother gave me his usual big brother smirk.

"Cranky, aren't we? When was the last time you slept?" Lincoln teased.

"I slept alright. Maybe not enough." I sighed, realizing how much I still needed his help. Without Lincoln, without Chloe, I was nothing but a woman chasing ghosts.

"You know, Kai is probably fine. Nothing would ever

happen to him without one of his bodyguards being there to stop it. That much I know."

"You don't know that." I said.

Lincoln shrugged and rolled his eyes—it was his "I know I'm right" look. Or was it his "I'm older, so you should listen to me" look? Either way, it was strangely comforting to see that expression again. I guessed that was what a big brother was for.

Lincoln probably thought he knew better than anyone, having been around him for so long I knew that's what he thought. But this time it felt different. Kai didn't seem like the same person I used to know. He was still playful when that side of him came through, but there was something else—something *heavier*—like he'd matured overnight. Or maybe it had happened over the three years we'd had no contact. Was that possible? Could people really change so much?

"What's your plan when you get to Shanghai now?" Chloe asked, pulling me from my thoughts.

"I don't know." A surge of guilt swept through me. I hadn't even thought about Dave and his team until now. How could I be so selfish?

"I was actually just going to follow Dave around. He'd know where to start looking for Kai." My voice cracked, and a fresh wave of tears pricked my eyes. "I don't know what happened to Dave. It's so fucking unbelievable— he's done everything to protect me, to help me, and all I could think about was myself."

"That's..." Chloe started but faltered, her mouth hanging open as if she couldn't find the words. She moved gracefully to my side, brushing her hand along my arm before wrapping me in a warm, reassuring hug.

"His life could be in danger for all I know," I whispered, guilt thick in my throat.

"When I called the airport, their security said no one had been arrested today. But they did mention some kind of filming happening—a group of influencers making short films," Chloe said softly.

I blinked at her, stunned. She had taken the initiative to check on Dave when I couldn't even pull myself together.

"What? Like an Instagram influencer?" I asked, barely processing the information.

"Apparently," Chloe replied, her voice light but her expression serious.

Lincoln excused himself, leaving Chloe and me alone in the kitchen.

I leaned against the counter, the weight of everything pressing down on me.

"We have to help Dave. Without Kai here, he's got no one," I said, though for all I knew, Dave might have a whole network of people supporting him in the U.S.

"Do you want me to call my cousin Marie?"

"The one married to the Mafia?" I asked weakly. The thought of the Mafia sent a chill through me.

"Funny story, actually," Chloe mused. "The old boss was Marie's father. He had an affair with her mother, and when his wife found out, she sent Matteo—her nephew —to kill Marie and her mom. But instead, Matteo fell in love with her."

I frowned. "Funny what some people consider funny."

My gut told me that story didn't have a happy ending for everyone involved. When I thought of the Mafia, all I could picture was bloodshed.

Then again, maybe people thought the same thing about doctors—we had plenty of blood on our hands, too.

"Oh sweetie, you're..." Chloe's voice softened as she tucked a stray lock of hair behind my ear, her touch gentle and familiar, like it had always been since we were kids.

"I'm what?" I challenged, narrowing my eyes. "Finish that sentence, I dare you."

"Innocent," she said simply, without a trace of teasing. "And it's not a bad thing. Look, if anyone could find Dave, it's the New York Mafia."

I exhaled shakily.

"I guess you're right." Deep down, I knew she was right—but that didn't make it easier to accept.

"They aren't bad people," Chloe insisted, her voice low and steady. "They just do things... differently. They won't hurt anyone—unless they have to."

Her voice dropped on the last words, a shadow crossing her face as if she'd seen the line between right and wrong blur more times than she cared to admit.

"Okay, fine. Whatever you think is best. Right now, I can't think straight." I finally admitted, exhaustion weight heavy in my bones. My mind spun with too many what-ifs, too many things I couldn't control.

"I know." Chloe squeezed my hand reassuringly. "Just

remember, you've got me and Lincoln. Whatever you need, you just say the word. And you can call anytime—I mean it. No matter what."

The warmth in her words cracked something inside me.

"Thanks Chlo, for everything." I meant it. Without Lincoln, I couldn't reach Kai.

And without Chloe and her powerful family, I had no way of helping Dave. I'd spent my entire career fixing people, but when it mattered most, I couldn't even help myself.

The helplessness gnawed at me, raw and unrelenting.

"Don't mention it. We'll do anything for you—you know that?" I nodded, my throat too tight to speak. "Besides, Dave's probably handled worse situations before. He's just a bodyguard. There's no reason for anyone to hurt him."

Her logic made sense, but it didn't ease the knot of dread twisting in my stomach. My heart thudded painfully against my ribs, each beat echoing with all the things I couldn't control.

Lincoln returned a few moments later, his phone pressed to his ear, his jaw tight. His tone was cool and businesslike—no trace of the earlier warmth.

"Do you have a visa for China?" he asked abruptly.

"What visa?" His question caught me off guard, my voice rising in confusion.

Lincoln gave me a long, disbelieving look as he continued his call. "No, she doesn't have a visa. I didn't think so."

He listened for a moment longer, muttered a few more words, then hung up with a sigh of exasperation.

"Go on—tell me off." I said, crossing my arms defensively.

"Do you know you need a visa to visit China?" he asked, irritation lacing his voice.

"I've been to China before. I didn't need one," I argued, though even as the words left my mouth, doubt crept in.

"Are you sure? I'm talking about mainland China— not Taiwan, Hong Kong, or any other territory. Don't get them confused."

I swallowed hard, realizing my mistake. Feeling like a giant idiot. One point to my big brother.

"Then no," I admitted quietly, the fight draining out of me.

"I thought so. How could you not think about something like this? You're an adult. You've travelled before. How did this not cross your mind?" His words cut sharper than I expected.

"All your life, you've had everything planned for you," Lincoln continued, his tone sharp. "You've never had to do anything on your own."

"That's not fair, Lincoln." I protested, a flare of defensiveness rising. "I knew about visas. I always checked. But lately... I've gotten used to having someone handle those things for me. Haven't you? Why else would you have an assistant or a secretary?"

Lincoln ignored my defense. "You wouldn't have made it on that flight yesterday. They wouldn't even let you check in."

Tears burned my eyes again. My grand plan to save Kai had been flawed from the start. Even without the fake airport security, I wouldn't have gotten anywhere. I'd been so desperate, so reckless. It was a miracle I'd even made it this far.

"I wasn't thinking," I admitted, my voice trembling. "I... I panicked—I just wanted to see him."

"You didn't make it easy for me to help you." My big brother snapped. "If you'd told me your plan, you and Dave would already be in China. Instead, you made reckless decisions and crashed your car. You could've died."

I had no defense left—only guilt and regret, twisting together in a painful knot.

"If Chloe hadn't had Raj following you, we wouldn't even know you were in danger. What am I supposed to do with you? Do you want me to fucking microchip you? You know I will." He slammed his fist against the kitchen island, the sound loud and final in the quiet room.

Chloe rested a calming hand on his arm. "We care about you. You scared the hell out of us."

My vision blurred as more tears streamed out. Despite everything, Chloe and Lincoln were still here, still willing to fight for me.

"My plane will take you to Hong Kong instead," Lincoln said, his tone shifting back to business.

"Hong Kong?" My stomach twisted at the thought of returning there. "How do I get over to Shanghai."

"You'll need... special documents." He said darkly.

I shivered at his tone. Whatever he had in mind, it wasn't going to be simple.

"Tell me more."

4

____

Kai

I closed my eyes as Mario sped through the Chen estate, tearing past the security gate without much resistance.

Nothing was going to stop me. Nothing was going to stop me. Nothing was going to stop me.

I repeated that mantra, steeling myself. Jenny was getting out. There was no question about it. Chen's men had been slow to respond, clearly underestimating us. They didn't think we had the guts to ram through the security gate—the same high-tech gate designed to keep intruders like us out. I had one myself. Yet, after only two hits, it crumpled. Maybe I had underestimated Mario's strategy.

Or maybe luck was on our side.

At the grand wooden entrance, a crowd of Chen's men waited. Their radios had surely spread the word that some crazy intruders were incoming. Mario stepped out, carrying a massive hunting rifle in hand, and motioned for me to follow.

No one dared move against us. Mario's reputation preceded him—the crazy Italian who thrived on confrontation. Armed with that rifle, only a fool would challenge him.

I didn't know how he got his hands on such a weapon. And I didn't care. When you know the right people, nothing is out of reach.

Then I noticed something else—some of Chen's men exchanged glances with Mario.

Recognition?

Familiarity?

He clearly knew them.

Maybe even had an agreement with them.

"Where to?" I tested my theory.

Mario's gaze flicked to a large woman in a group. She arched a brow and tilted her head.

"Upstairs," I announced, catching the faint shouting coming from the floor above.

Without hesitation, I sprinted up the marble staircase, Mario close behind. Jenny's voice grew louder with every step, her screams echoing through the corridor.

No guards.

No one to stop us.

I found her instantly. Her bedroom door stood wide open. She was in the middle of the room, screaming, hurling a yellow leather bag to the floor.

"What the hell are you doing here?" Chen's voice cut through the chaos. His surprise was genuine. Did none of his men warn him?

I stood by the doorway, staring at him, then Jenny's tear-streaked face.

"Come with me," I said, extending a hand towards Jenny.

Chen sneered, stepping between us. "Get the fuck out. This is none of your business."

"I hate you!" Jenny shrieked. Her body trembled as tears streamed down her face. She flung a jewelry box against the wall, shards scattering across the floor. "Why do you always do this to me."

"Honey, I love you." Chen said, his tone oozing a forced sweetness.

"Lies. All you care about is your reputation."

"Of course, I care about you. You're my wife."

"And what about your mistresses? You think I don't know about them?"

"They mean nothing. All they get is money and a dirty fuck."

Jenny laughed bitterly, her voice cracking. "I should never have believed you. All you do is hurt me."

Chen's face darkened. "Don't be ungrateful. What about the life I gave you? The jewelry, designer bags, the surgeries to keep you young and beautiful?"

"Same goes for your whores."

"But I come home to you. You get to be Mrs. Chen."

"I've heard enough," she spat.

Her eyes found mine. "Jenny, let's go already."

"She's my wife. You have no right to take her."

"I'm not taking her," I said coldly. "You're the one who took her by force, remember? She's leaving if she wants to."

Chen's face twisted in rage. "She belongs to me. She's my wife, my property. I can do whatever I want with her."

"You're out of your mind. Wake up. This isn't ancient China. You don't own anyone."

"Not when you're me."

I turned to Jenny. "Tell him you want a divorce."

"I want a divorce." Her lips trembled, but her voice was clear.

"Not a chance."

"I want a divorce." She repeated, louder this time. The fear in her eyes burned into fury.

"Say it again," Chen challenged.

"I. Want. A. Divorce."

The slap came so fast I barely saw it. Jenny collapsed to the floor. Chen grabbed her by the ponytail, yanked her upright, and struck her again.

Rage blinded me. I lunged at him, but his blows came just as quick. By the time I reached him, he had already kicked Jenny twice in the stomach.

Mario surged forward, locking Chen in a chokehold. I drove my fist into his face, then his gut. Each punch landed with a sickening crunch, but it wasn't enough to stop him. Chen thrashed violently in Mario's grip, his rage boiling over.

His scream pierced the air—but not from my punch.

"What the fuck do you think you're doing?" Chen's voice cracked with fury.

I turned.

Jenny stood frozen, a bloodied utility knife in her trembling hand. Her knuckles were white from gripping the blade too tightly, her chest rising and falling in frantic bursts.

"Qing Qing," I said softly, using her nickname like a lifeline. My heart slammed against my ribs. "Put the knife down."

Her wild, tear-filled eyes met mine. Pain and defiance burned in her gaze.

"I'm done," she whispered. Her voice hollow and broken. And then, before I could stop her, she dragged the blade down her inner her wrist in one swift motion.

"No!" I shouted, my blood turning ice-cold.

Blood poured from the deep gash, dripping down her arm and staining the pale silk of her dress. She staggered back, her breathing ragged, her face pale as death.

Chen roared with rage, his strength surging as he wrenched free from Mario's grasp. He lunged toward her, his palm cracking against her cheek with enough force to twist her head to the side.

Jenny screamed as he raised his hand for another blow. His face twisted with nothing but hatred.

I couldn't stop the slap—it came too fast. But I tackled him to the ground before he could strike her again.

We crashed hard, the air bursting from my lungs as we hit the marble floor. Jenny crumpled beside us, blood soaking the hem of her dress and pooling beneath her. My fists landed hard, raw anger driving every punch. But Chen didn't flinch. His eyes burned with madness as he reached for her again.

"Bitch, you think you can threaten me like that?" he roared, his voice thick with venom. He clawed at Jenny, grabbing a fistful of her hair and jerking her toward him.

"Let her go!" My voice was a snarl, but he didn't listen.

His hand cracked against her face again. And again. Each slap echoed through the room, and with every blow, something inside me snapped.

Mario tried to pull him off. But Chen was a possessed man—driven by an uncontrollable need to punish Jenny for defying him. He didn't care about the blood or the consequences—only his control. His grip tightened in her hair, and Jenny let out a pained whimper as fresh tears streamed down her cheeks.

I threw a savage punch into his side, hearing the sharp crack of a rib giving way. He bellowed in pain, his body shuddering. But he didn't stop.

He couldn't stop.

Then, just as suddenly, everything stopped.

I froze, my heart pounding in my chest as I watched blood gushing out of Chen's throat.

"Bitch." Cheng managed to squeeze the word out, his voice a rasping croak.

"I wouldn't talk if I were you." Jenny crawled away from Chen as his monstrous hold finally loosened. Slowly, she pulled herself up and stood over her husband.

The knife slipped from her trembling hand, clattering to the floor. She wobbled as she moved, leaving a smeared trail of blood behind her. After picking up a pink dress from a nearby chair, she turned and walked towards me.

"Should I die with him?" Jenny gave me a faint smile, her tear-streaked face pale and hollow.

"No," I responded, finally snapping out of my daze.

I stood and guided Jenny to sit down on the bed. Tearing the pink dress she handed me, I wrapped the fabric tightly around her wrist. The cut was deep—too deep. I sandwiched my wrist between my hands, applying as much pressure as I could to slow the bleeding.

The room fell into a heavy, tense silence.

Mario had gone downstairs. I knew he would do whatever was required. I had no other option but to trust him at a time like this.

Jenny slumped against me, resting her face on my shoulder. Her crying had never really stopped since I stepped into the room. It had ebbed and flowed, but the tears kept coming—an endless, broken stream.

"What are we going to do now?" she whispered, her voice barely audible.

I glanced over at Chen, lying motionless in a pool of his own blood. His hand trembled weakly against his throat in a futile attempt to stop the bleeding. Despite the gaping wound, his face twisted with a mixture of shock and rage—like he couldn't believe what Jenny had done and wanted her to pay for it.

What happened? I searched my memory, but the moment was a blur. I had been too busy prying him off Jenny—I hadn't even seen her strike the fatal blow.

But there was no denying the truth. He wasn't going to make it. Jenny had killed her husband. Her abuser.

"What did you do?" I needed to hear it from her. I needed to know that it was self-defense.

"I didn't mean to," she murmured, shaking her head.

"We have to call the police." As much as I wanted him

dead, I knew that keeping him alive—if even possible—was a better solution.

"They'll think I murdered him," she said bitterly.

"He was hurting you." I pointed out, my voice sharp with frustration.

"So... you punched him." Her gaze locked onto mine, reminding me of my own role in this disaster.

"I couldn't just stand there..."

The images flashed through my mind—Chen dragging Jenny by her hair, his hand cracking across her face. The slapping noise filling the air of the room. I shook my head, trying to push them away.

"You kicked him." Jenny added quietly.

"I did." My chest tightened. This wasn't the first time he had hurt her, and it killed me that I hadn't been there to protect her.

"You could get into trouble if we called the police."

"I would kick him again if I had to." I didn't hesitate. I would protect her—no matter the consequences.

"If you let me bleed to death, you could tell the police that you found us like this. I killed him, and then I killed myself." Her voice was chillingly calm. "I'll take all the blame."

"No." I snapped. "Stop talking like that. Have you thought about your children? The baby you're carrying?"

"Yes, of course. I think about them every single day." Her voice cracked with pain. I knew she loved them deeply—no matter what anyone else believed. She hadn't abandoned them out of selfishness. She had left to survive.

"Mario... Mario will know what to do." The words felt

hollow, but I clung to them. Right now, I had no better ideas. I tried to keep my composure, but my lips trembled as I spoke.

I had done my fair share of terrible things. But I had never got my hands dirty—not like this. Paying someone else to handle the mess had always been my way. But this? This was something else entirely.

"It would be easier if I die with him." Jenny said quietly.

"No." My throat tightened. "Please stop that. It was self-defense."

"Was it?" Her smile sent an icy chill through me—a smile that belonged in a horror movie.

"It was? I saw it with my own eyes. Everyone here can testify for you—Mario included. The guards and the housekeeper must've seen what he did."

"They can only prove that I was assaulted," she said. "But bruises don't have names. Everyone will think I killed him for the money."

"That's ridiculous."

"No, it isn't." Her laugh was bitter. "My family's been drowning in debt for years. That's why they made me marry him in the first place—hoping his family connections would save my father's crumbling empire."

"I... I thought you loved him."

"I did. For the first few years." Her voice softened. "I was naive. I thought I'd found the perfect husband."

"That's what you made everyone believe," I said quietly. "You seemed so happy."

"I was. And then... I wasn't."

A faint sound interrupted us.

"Help..." Chen's voice, weak and broken.

"We should help him," I declared, guilt gnawing at my chest.

I should have helped him before. But the truth was, I cared more about Jenny. Her life mattered more to me.

"Let's wait another minute." Jenny murmured, her words sending another chill down my spine.

On the floor lay the husband she had once loved. The father of her children. The man she had tried to win back, time and again.

"Qing Qing." I whispered, using her childhood nickname again—a desperate plea.

She wrapped her arms around my waist. "Please."

One. Two. Three...

I counted silently, the seconds dragging by. When I reached sixty, I moved to Chen's side. Tearing off my sleeve, I pressed it against his throat, trying to stem the flow of blood.

"Stay with me. Stay with me, you bastard," I muttered.

Chen let out a faint, familiar smile—the kind reserved for trusted friends. It twisted something deep inside me.

Mario returned, his face hard. "Give me your phone."

"Can't you see I'm a little busy?" I snapped.

Without a word, he frisked my pocket, pulled out my phone, and slammed it to the floor. The screen shattered under his boot.

"What the fuck, Mario?"

"It's what they do in the movies," he said with a shrug. "Don't want them tracking us."

Idiot. That was who I had to rely on.

"Grab me a towel—he's soaking through..." I barked.

"Why? We should just watch him die." His tone was casual, but the words were ice-cold.

He returned with a towel, tossing it to me.

I padded the towel on top of the bloody sleeve.

"Call an ambulance," I ordered.

"Why?" Mario protested.

"Because you broke mine."

"It should come from me." Jenny's voice was quiet but firm. She pulled her phone from her blood-soaked dress, her fingers trembling as she held it. For a second, she just sat there, staring at the screen like she was weighing every possible outcome. Then, with a sharp breath, she hit the green button.

"Help," she cried, her voice raw with panic. "Please, my husband—he hit me, and now he'd bleeding everywhere. Please come, hurry!"

She dropped the phone with a dramatic finality, her performance chillingly perfect.

"Unbelievable," I muttered under my breath.

Chen was too weak to even say another word at this point. His breaths came in shallow gasps, his lips trembling as blood pooled around him.

"Don't fall asleep," I said sharply, shaking him as though sheer force of will could keep him alive.

Jenny turned to face me.

"I couldn't take it anymore," she said, her voice hollow. "Years. I've spent years enduring his anger, his fists. Every time he hurt me, I told myself I could survive it. That it would get better. That if I was just patient enough, he would change. But he didn't."

Her hands trembled at her sides, her nails digging into her palms.

"He always promised he would stop, but the beatings got worse. The words got sharper. And I—" Her voice cracked. "I became someone I didn't even recognize. Scared. Weak."

She laughed bitterly, a sound too hollow to carry any warmth. "It had to end eventually. One way or another. Either I died, or he did, or maybe both of us. There was no other way out."

A shiver ran down my spine at the rawness of her words. I had known Jenny for most of my life, but I had never seen her like this—so broken.

"No one ever really saw it," she continued, "not my family, not my friends. I smiled for the world because that's what a good wife does, right? You hide the bruises. You hide the fear. But behind closed doors... she made sure I never forgot who had the power. Every slap, every broken bone, every time he threatened to take my children away..."

Her body swayed, weak from blood loss and the weight of her confession.

"Tonight... tonight was the last time. He wasn't going to stop. And if I hadn't done it—" Her voice dropped to a whisper. "He would have killed me."

"Jenny..." I reached for her, but she shook her head.

"I didn't mean to kill him," she said softly, tears began to fall again, "you have to believe me. I just wanted him to stop. I wanted him to be afraid. To know that I have the power to stand up for myself."

"Don't worry, boss," Mario said, his voice cutting

through the heaviness of Jenny's words. "I talked to the staff. They know what to say."

"We did nothing wrong," I insisted, though the words tasted like a lie in my mouth.

"Doesn't look like it," his reply a little too quick before realizing he had spoken too soon.

5

June

Wendy and I stood in front of a four-foot-wide desk. It squeaked every time the slender woman behind it made even the tiniest movement. Its wonky legs protested under the workload they'd endured over the years. After a few long minutes, the bleached blonde finally looked up at me and let out a loud, exaggerated sigh.

"Sorry, can't help you," she said matter-of-factly.

This was the fourth place we'd been to—and the last one.

After all, getting a fake travel document for China wasn't exactly a business you could find advertised on the internet. Lincoln's guy couldn't help us. And through Wendy's seemingly suspicious yet surprisingly effective connections, we had managed to track down three more places that weren't even on Lincoln's radar.

"Do you know anywhere else I can go?" I asked, trying to keep the desperation out of my voice.

"Well, to be honest..." She paused as the banging from next door grew faster, accompanied by a melodic moan that could rival the best internet starlet.

"No one will help you," she finished, only after the masseuse and her client had finally calmed down.

"Why?" Wendy tilted her head, folding her arms over her large chest. "We can pay you more. Just name your price."

"It's not about the money." She took a slow drag from the cigarette in her hand and blew a cloud of smoke right in my face. "*It's her!*"

I held my breath, trying to avoid inhaling the second-hand smoke. The room fell into an uneasy silence—well, as silent as it could be with the occasional moans still echoing down the hall. I didn't need to look up to know that both Wendy and the fake blonde were staring at me, waiting for a confession I wasn't about to give.

"Thank you for your help." Politely, I placed some cash on the messy pile of Hong Kong identity cards.

"I didn't do anything," she said, pushing the cash away before taking another deep drag from her cigarette.

"You can keep it."

"Take your money, bitch." The fake IDs and a few lighter objects bounced as she slammed her fist against the old desk. "Sorry... I don't want any trouble, *ah-sou.*"

She stood abruptly and bowed, her dark brown eyes even darker—filled with a quiet, desperate plea for me to leave her and her business alone.

I stayed still, watching her tremble slightly as she took

another sharp inhale. Whoever had warned her off wasn't just issuing empty threats. Fear clung to her like a thick cloud of smoke in the room. This wasn't about greed or pride, this was survival.

And I was a problem she wanted gone.

"I'm not asking you to—"

"*Please.*" The word slipped out before she could stop it, low and shaky. She wasn't just refusing. She was scared. And whoever was behind it—whoever had shut down every option I found—was someone she didn't dare cross.

I stuffed the cash back into the pocket of my hoodie and left without another word.

No thanks. No goodbye. No more begging for help.

I walked out of the massage parlor and hurried away from the block of old, run-down shops. A hand grabbed the back of my elbow, making me jump.

"Slow down."

It was just Wendy.

I was okay.

"Sorry," I half mouthed, half whispered.

Wendy kept a firm grip on my elbow, gently steering me away from the middle of the sidewalk. People in Kowloon didn't walk as fast as the New Yorkers, but they weren't shy about giving you a hard, judgmental once-over—or barking out a curt, unfriendly *hey* if you were in their way.

"Let's go inside, I can do with one of those," Wendy said, nodding towards the rows of egg custard tarts displayed behind a glass cupboard.

My feet followed Wendy into the run-down cafe,

which sold nothing but Chinese egg tarts and a few cold beverages. The air was thick with the scent of butter and sugar—comforting, but far from calming.

After a loud back-and-forth exchange of broken English mixed with Mandarin and Cantonese, an old lady finally handed Wendy a brown box.

Wendy flipped it open the moment as she paid.

"Keep the change," she said, crumbs falling from her mouth as she spoke. With one hand on the box and the other gripping a half-eaten tart, there was no way she could take the change anyway. "This is the real deal—way better than the ones from Chinatown."

The elderly couple behind the counter bustled around, serving a few passersby and greeting regulars by name. But their attention never fully left us. We settled at one of the two small tables available—not that we had much choice, one table was occupied by their makeshift workstation, piled with flattened boxes waiting to be folded.

Their eyes darted over to us every so often, as if to figure out why we were there. They must have been in their seventies, or maybe late sixties. When they weren't serving customers, the wife folded boxes while the husband scrolled idly through his phone. Yet, every time our eyes met, they offered us the same polite, awkward nod.

"I'm ready whenever you are," Wendy said, biting into her second egg tart. But the relaxed tone in her voice told me we weren't leaving anytime soon.

I exhaled a long, heavy sigh. "Well...I suspect my ex is behind all this."

"Fu–" Wendy reluctantly put down her new favorite food and gulped down some water to calm her cough. "Who the fuck are you, woman?"

She screwed the cap back onto the bottle of mineral water she'd stolen from the airline catering cart this morning.

I glanced up, and our eyes met. There were questions in her gaze—I could see that—but there was more. Concern and worry, I guessed, maybe even a hint of judgement, though I couldn't be sure.

Like her, I was feeling all those things, and more. I was worried about Kai, Lucy, Jenny, Dave and his team. I felt useless for begging my brother for help. Incompetent for needing Wendy to babysit me. And exposed—because my past, the part no one knew about, was about to be laid bare.

Could I trust her?

Would she report everything back to Lincoln and Chloe?

Most likely.

"I dated this guy..." The words came out slowly as I weighed my options—or rather, the consequences of not telling Wendy anything.

"Spill now, or I walk."

There it was. I had no other choice.

"It's a long story."

"Just tell me the short version." Wendy stuffed a custard tart into my hand before helping herself to another one.

"My ex... he's the head of the largest and most

powerful triad in Hong Kong." I peeled off a flaky piece of pastry and nibbled on it.

She nodded, raising her eyebrows, urging me to continue.

"I think he's behind everything."

"You mean you think he has Kai?"

"No, I don't think so." I shook my head, then froze as Wendy's question finally caught up with my thoughts. "Wait—you don't think…? Oh God, I hope not. Mack works for Dannie."

Wendy plucked the custard tart from my hand, as she finished off her third. "Let's assume this Dannie boy has nothing to do with Kai's disappearance. Because no triad boss would risk kidnapping a billionaire for a scumbag like Mack, right?"

That was exactly what I had been telling myself. The Dannie I knew wouldn't do something that reckless—or at least the Dannie I knew back then.

"Right." I nodded eagerly. "I think he's the reason those people won't help us with the fake documents—but I don't know why…"

"Just you, honey. I've got my travel documents." Wendy brushed the crumbs from her hands and the front of her yellow floral t-shirt, then wiped her mouth and fingers with a wet tissue she pulled from her backpack.

"I don't know what to do." I whispered, glancing outside at the people passing by.

"You do." Wendy's eyebrows furrowed as she looked over at me, before she took another drink from her water bottle.

I did know what to do. Dannie wanted something from me. I just had to figure out what and give it to him.

"Maybe."

"Why didn't you tell me you knew that woman?"

"What woman?"

"The one who called you some Chinese nickname." Wendy narrowed her eyes. "Please—I might be jet-lagged and starving, but don't think I'm not paying attention, lady. Let me tell you, the hungrier I get, the more awake I am. Got it?"

And cranky too.

"What did she call me?" I asked, my mind racing. She might have been awake and alert, but I was freaking out —and apparently not paying enough attention.

"Sounded like *Aso*."

I made a noise—something between a cough and a laugh—but had no idea what to say.

"*Ah sou*." The old woman answered nonchalantly from behind the counter. "It means she's married to the boss."

I froze. It struck me then—how strange it was she hadn't spoken a single word of English when Wendy struggled to order the tarts. And all this time, it had never crossed my mind that the cafe owners might understand us. Why should they? We weren't in America. And they'd understood everything. Every single word.

"You're married?" Wendy's voice cut through the haze of my thoughts.

"Not exactly. We just did this... cultural ceremony thing." My head bobbed side to side in an awkward attempt to downplay it.

The old woman snorted, a dry, knowing sound.

"*Haih*, that's considered married in the eyes of our gods and ancestors. And everyone." She chuckled softly, like she was humoring a naive child who didn't understand how the world worked.

"Not legally. We didn't sign anything."

"Maybe so," she said with a shrug, "but you'll always be his wife in our eyes."

Wendy's words shot out like a bullet. "You know him?"

The woman tilted her head, giving Wendy a look that suggested the answer was obvious. "Who doesn't know him around here? Every month, we pay him protection fees. And before him, his father—then his grandfather."

We hurriedly left the tart shop when I realized the owners knew Dannie.

It struck me then—they weren't the only ones. With that thought, the weight of unseen eyes settled on me. An eerie sensation crawled up my spine, prickling every nerve along the way.

Kai and my brother had people watching over me before. Their so-called security team had always been discreet—comforting, even. But this... this felt different. Unsettling.

Wendy still had questions—I could feel them hanging in the air, thick and heavy. Her stern stare burned into the side of my face, and I kept my eyes fixed ahead, avoiding hers. I wasn't an overly private person, but there were certain things I preferred to keep to myself.

"What do you want to do next?"

Funny that she should ask. Wasn't she the one who supposedly had all the answers? My brother and Chloe certainly seemed to think so.

"You tell me! You're the one with all the connections."

"What do you mean?"

I rolled my eyes, irritation prickling at the edges of my patience.

"I don't know," I snapped. "Check your little black book—maybe you've got a contact in the black market, or a mafia boss who owes you a favor."

"Fuck you."

"Thank you very much. Fuck you, too."

We marched down the street, power-walking with no real destination. If my pace got any faster, I'd be jogging. Wendy trailed beside me, her steps quick and deliberate, matching my speed. She didn't push—didn't press me for answers. Instead, she followed quietly, like a patient mother waiting for her stroppy teenager to burn off an unreasonable tantrum.

Except I wasn't the tantrum-throwing type.

Well... that was a lie.

My version of a tantrum was quieter—subtle enough that no one usually noticed. But right now? Right now, I wasn't sure I could hide it.

I didn't know exactly how I was feeling. But it felt good—almost freeing—to finally let my emotions out. To be angry. To be scared.

"Can we slow down?" Wendy asked at last, her voice breaking the tense silence.

I had no idea how to pull us out of the awkward moment I'd created by snapping at her. Bless her beautiful soul for not walking away. We came to a stop at a busy crossroad, standing beside a group of students in crisp uniforms. They laughed and chatted, each holding an ice cream cone or a cup of boba tea, blissfully unaware of the storm swirling inside me.

"I thought this would be easy," Wendy continued, brushing a stray hair from her face. "But this... this is out of my hands."

Her words cut through me like a knife.

"So, does that mean you're going to leave me?" My voice trembled despite my best efforts to keep it steady.

"No, of course not." She hesitated, biting her lip.

"May... may—" she stuttered, struggling to find the right words, "maybe we should both walk away from this. Leave this place."

"Leave Kai?" I turned to face her fully, scanning her expression for any sign that she was joking—or losing her mind.

"Yes, and no," she replied softly. "Maybe we could go home and get help from there."

"Going home means losing time, Wendy. Kai could be in real danger." My heart pounded harder at the thought. Every second felt like it could be the difference between saving him—or being too late.

"I know," she sighed. "But my friends—our friends—are back home. My contacts here... they're not as deep as you think."

I exhaled a heavy sigh, the weight of our helplessness pressing against my chest. "I'm sorry for what I said. I didn't mean it. I don't even know what I was thinking."

Her expression softened. "But you obviously know someone here."

Her large brown eyes locked onto mine, searching—waiting. The urge to confess swelled inside me, pushing against the walls I'd built around the truth.

"I wish I could tell you everything," I said, my voice barely above a whisper. "But there's no time."

As reluctant as I felt, Wendy had put herself on the line to protect me. I owed her at least the basics—the truth she needed to fully understand what we were really up against.

She reached out and gave my hand a reassuring squeeze. "You can trust me."

A gust of wind hit me square in the face—because, of course, it did. If this were a movie, this would be the moment where the hero or heroine faced the truth—the kind of truth that had always been their biggest problem of their life.

Trust issues.

I never pretended to be a perfect person. And as if my list of flaws wasn't long enough, Wendy had just added a new one to it.

"It's not that I don't trust you."

I lied.

Ten seconds ago, it wouldn't have felt like a lie. It would've rolled off my tongue naturally—sounding convincing, at least to myself. And, at that point, it would've been true. I hadn't even realized that I didn't trust Wendy. Or anyone, for that matter.

Was that normal? Did other people feel like that?

"I get it." Wendy's warm hand slid onto my shoulder,

her fingers moving in slow, comforting strokes. "I know we don't really know each other."

"We don't."

"I'm only here as a favor to Rox—well Chloe."

"That's right." My voice sharpened despite myself. See? My trust issues weren't irrational—she had just admitted she wasn't there for me.

"Don't we all do things we don't want to for people we love?"

Her bluntness hit me harder than the wind, landing with a sting no breeze could match.

I dipped my head in a small nod, unsure how to respond. "You didn't have to come."

"Actually, I didn't want to come in the first place."

Ouch.

"Then why are you here?" My voice came out quieter than I intended, the words laced with a vulnerability I couldn't quite hide.

"Can we get a boba? I'm thirsty."

I blinked at her sudden change of subject. "Drink your water—boba isn't going to hydrate you."

"I want a boba." She crossed her arms defiantly. "I'm getting a boba whether you like it or not."

And just like that, the tension cracked—if only a little.

I hated her for wasting my time. Fantasies flickered through my mind—sprinting down the back alley, flagging down a random taxi, even stealing a motorcycle from a stranger. Any escape would do. But instead, I stayed rooted to the spot, waiting as Wendy strolled toward the boba shop with an inflatable snowman bobbing beside the entrance.

When she came back, her face was lit up with a big self-satisfied grin. She dug into her latest conquest—a brown sugar sundae—spooning white, velvety ice cream dotted with black tapioca pearls into her mouth.

"This has to be my new favorite sundae."

"I thought you wanted a drink."

She pointed with her spoon toward the sealed plastic cup tucked securely in the cup holder hanging off the side of her bag.

"Got one. Multitasking, babe."

I rolled my eyes, biting back the urge to snap. Time was slipping away, and she was acting like we were on a carefree vacation.

"I used to think you were boring."

Her words caught me off guard. My head snapped towards her. "Excuse me?"

"Yeah, you know," she said casually, scooping up another bite. "You grew up in that perfect little family. Your doctor family... all prestigious and proper. If you were a real white bitch, I would've totally ignored you."

"You can't say that—it's racist."

"Oh, come on. We're not in America. People with money have it easy, and bonus points if you're white. But I know you're mixed or something, and you lived in New York, so I guess that evens things out."

I scoffed under my breath. She had no idea how many patients had walked out on me the moment they realized my face didn't match my surname.

"Your point being?"

I glanced down, brushing my sleeve over my wrist in a

subtle, impatient gesture—only to realize I wasn't even wearing a watch. Perfect.

"Well, when I heard about your dirty little secret at the dirty little tart shop," Wendy said, shoveling another heaping spoonful of ice cream into her mouth, "ohh la la, turns out you're a naughty girl. That's when I decided this trip might actually be worth my while."

I rolled my eyes. "So, you're here for what? Gossip?"

"No. Maybe a little." She grinned, unbothered by my irritation. "But all that drama makes you interesting. And that means I actually like you now."

"Perfect, why don't I feel like that's a compliment?"

"It doesn't?" She blinked innocently.

"No."

"Well, it should." With a flourish, she tossed the empty plastic cup into the trash outside the shop, as if she had just solved all our problems.

"Can we get on with our day?" My tone came out sharper than I intended—impatient, clipped. A tone I knew all too well, no doubt inherited from my own mother.

Wendy, of course, wasn't fazed. "Well, if you'd just open your little black book, maybe you'd already have that travel document by now."

She shrugged, her voice light and teasing but with an edge of seriousness. "But if you don't want to, maybe we should focus on finding a hotel first. Get some rest, clear our heads a little—"

Her voice faded into a rambling monologue, a stream of words I barely registered.

One thing, however, stood out. We had landed and

rushed straight out of the airport without giving a single thought to accommodations. In my mind, getting a fake ID was supposed to be quick—like one of those one-hour photo places back home. I hadn't planned on staying here longer than half a day.

But we couldn't afford to waste any more time.

Without hesitation, I stepped to the curb and waved down a red cab flashing a vacant sign.

"Where are we going?" Wendy asked, sliding into the cab.

"Just get in." I ducked under the doorframe and followed her inside.

"I'm so glad you finally agreed to go to a hotel," she quipped, her voice dripping with sarcasm.

I ignored her and leaned forward, speaking to the driver in my best attempt at Cantonese. "Kamsha Dai Ha."

The driver twisted around, his weathered face shifting between me and Wendy before his eyes narrowed in suspicion.

"Where you going?" he asked, his tone sharp.

I repeated myself, slower this time. "Kam. Sha. Dai. Ha."

The old man sucked his teeth and let out a sound that resembled an annoyed "*hiya.*" After a heavy pause, he grumbled something under his breath, then shifted the cab into gear and pulled into traffic.

"What's his problem." Wendy muttered, watching the city blur past the window.

"Well..." I hesitated, "The place we're going—it's

supposed to be the most haunted building in all of Hong Kong."

Her head snapped toward me. "What? Why?"

Before I could answer, the driver cut in, his voice gruff. "I also ask you why."

He jabbed a finger toward the rearview mirror, his expression a mix of disbelief and concern. "You go in... you don't come out."

His words hung heavy in the air and I wasn't sure if he was trying to scare us or if he genuinely believed it.

The drive only took ten minutes, but each passing second stretched unbearably long. I stole a glance at Wendy, wondering if she was rattled. She looked calm—too calm—but I couldn't tell if that was bravado or genuine indifference.

Meanwhile, the driver quietly chanted under his breath. "*O-Nei-Tou-Fat... O-Nei-Tou-Fat...*" The repetitive rhythm prickled my nerves. If I remembered correctly—thanks to the endless Kung Fu movies my brothers forced me to sit through—it was a Buddhist mantra meant to ward off evil spirits. Comforting.

When the cab finally jerked to a stop, the driver didn't bother to hide his relief. "You're here."

His knuckles were white against the steering wheel.

I looked out the window at the looming shadow of Kamsha Dai Ha. Even in the daylight, the building seemed to pulse with an eerie, unwelcoming energy.

"How much is it?" I asked, pulling out two one-hundred notes—more than enough to cover the fare.

"You know what? Just keep the change."

Instead of taking the money, the driver shoved my

hand away, his face pale. "I don't want your money. If you die inside, don't come looking for me."

"Cheery," Wendy quipped, because of course. She couldn't help herself. I was beginning to realize that no matter the situation—whether it was life-threatening or just plain awkward—her instinct was always to crack a joke.

"I'm sorry." The rasp in the driver's voice, paired with slight tremor, sent a chill crawling up my spine. His fear wasn't an act—it was raw, real, and contagious. The moment our doors slammed shut, he stomped on the gas, peeling away like the devil himself was at his heels.

We stood in silence, staring up at the decaying tower looming before us.

The building was as uninviting as the driver's warning. Its once-white facade was now a patchwork of grime and neglect. The foyer's outer walls were smeared with graffiti—some of it crude drawings of penises, others angry Chinese scrawled in blood-red paint.

"Fuck," Wendy muttered, her voice low but sharp. "This place definitely looks haunted."

Her already large eyes widened even further, pupils blown dark with something between awe and unease.

"You scared?" I asked, though the words barely left my throat.

She grinned. "I'm excited."

Of course, she was.

6

———

June

The building was as run-down as I remembered —maybe even worse. Then again, how do you measure the decay of a place that was already a dump to begin with?

What the driver said wasn't entirely true. Some people *did* live here. Despite the city's obsession with ghosts stories, there were always a few who didn't buy into the whole haunted-building myth. But superstition wasn't the real reason people stayed away from Kam Sha. No, the truth was far simpler—and far more dangerous. Staying here without permission could cost you an arm, a leg, or even your life.

I led the way into a dimly lit hallway, the flickering fluorescent light above humming faintly. At the end of the corridor, we stopped in front of the building's only working elevator—if you could call it that. The up and down buttons were grimy, worn smooth by years of use.

As we waited, the silence settled heavy around us, broken only by the distant grinding of machinery and the muffled noise of the city outside.

For once, Wendy was quiet. And oddly enough, I missed her sarcastic commentary.

With a loud, metallic groan, the elevator finally arrived. Its dented steel door screeched open, revealing a cramped, yellowed interior. The air inside was thick and stale, carrying the unmistakable stench of urine and cigarette smoke.

Wendy wrinkled her nose, tiptoeing in like she could avoid the invisible filth. "Ugh. Someone really couldn't wait."

I stepped inside, turning to face the rusted control panel. Rows of faded buttons glowed weakly under the dim light.

"Which floor is it?" she asked.

"Eighteenth." I pressed the '17' button, feeling Wendy's gaze burning into me.

Her brows furrowed in confusion.

"Then why—"

"Just trust me."

The door groaned shut, trapping us in the eerie silence.

Wendy groaned in agreement, watching me carefully.

"Are you nervous?" I should have been. But I wasn't sure I had the luxury of fear anymore.

I was nervous—but admitting it wouldn't help either of us. Instead, I shrugged, lifting my shoulders to their highest point before letting them drop. I repeated the motion a few more times, as if it could shake off the growing tension crawling under my skin.

Ding.

The elevator shuddered to a stop at 3A. The metal doors slid open with a reluctant groan. There was nobody on the other side. The doors closed and the elevator shuddered again as it started to climb.

"What was that?" Wendy whispered, her voice tight.

"It always does that." I kept my tone flat, unwilling to let her hear the unease creeping in.

She flinched, rubbing her arms as goosebumps spread across her skin. "Don't your people think the number four is, like, super unlucky?"

"I wouldn't know." I lied.

Wendy fell silent again, but her hand didn't stop moving—the faint sound of her boba straw scraping against plastic filled the heavy air.

Ding.

This time, we both jumped. My heart slammed against my ribs.

The doors creaked open at 13A—a floor the elevator had never stopped at before. A chill swept through the air as the gap widened, and this time, the doors didn't close right away.

They stayed open... too long.

"I think I see someone." Wendy's voice barely rose above a breath.

I followed her gaze—and there it was. A shadow at the far end of the dim corridor. Small. Pale. Dressed in white. And moving.

My stomach twisted.

"Fuck," Wendy hissed, her body tensing beside me.

The figured shifted, inching closer.

"It's coming towards us. Close the door—*close it!*"

My hands refused to move. My brain screamed at them, but my fingers stayed frozen, useless.

"It's a child…" The words slipped out before I could stop them. "What is a kid doing here?"

Wendy had taken over, jabbing the 'close' button like her life depended on it.

"It's coming toward us." Her voice trembled, raw with panic.

"Maybe *it* needs help." I slapped her hand away from the panel—ignoring the sting in my palm—and stepped forward, ready to exit.

Before I could move, Wendy yanked me back just as the door groaned shut.

"What the fuck do you think you're doing?" Her breath came fast, harsh against the stale air.

"How can you be so selfish? That boy—or girl— might need help. Have you even looked around?" My chest burned with frustration. I didn't specialize in fertility medicine by accident—I loved kids. I wanted one of my own someday. The thought of a child left alone in a place like this… it tore at something deep inside me.

"Yes, I've seen it. Thank you *very* much." Wendy's stone sharpened to a blade. She gestured at the cracked walls, the peeling paint, the graffiti scrawled in angry, jagged strokes. "Have you seen this place? This place is a goddamn nightmare. It could be a trap—you know that, right? Have you seriously never watched a horror movie?"

"This isn't a horror movie."

"Well, it might as well be."

Before I could fire back, a mechanical *ding* cut through the argument—the elevator arriving at 17. The doors rumbled open, revealing a long corridor swallowed by shadows.

"Now what?"

"This is as far as it goes."

"Please don't tell me we have to walk in there," she muttered, her usual sarcasm falling flat against the weight of the moment.

I shook my head. "No." My fingers hovered over the worn buttons. "Now I put in the password."

I pressed 2—waited precisely two seconds—then 7. Another pause. Finally, 15.

"Is this it?"

"This is it," I whispered.

Nothing happened.

"Are you sure?" Wendy asked.

I nodded, swallowing the rising lump in my throat. "I'm sure."

I punched the buttons again—2, 7, 15—with the same precision. Nothing.

"What are we going to do now?"

"I don't know." My voice broke on the last word as I wiped the tears that spilled without warning, hot and unwelcome. I cupped my hands over my mouth, trying to steady my breathing.

"I'm not walking out there." Wendy's words were firm, but I could hear the tremor hiding beneath them.

"I don't know what do to." The confession slipped out

before I could stop it. My vision blurred, the weight of everything pressing down all at once.

Without a word, Wendy wrapped her arms around me. I collapsed into her shoulder—warm, steady and comforting in a way I hadn't realized I needed.

A few moments passed with nothing but the faint hum of the elevator filling the silence between us.

"Are you sure your ex still lives here?" she whispered, her breath warm against my hair.

And there it was—the question I had been too scared to ask myself. What if Dannie didn't live here anymore? What if he had moved on? There were other ways to find them. Hell, we could've asked the old couple at the tart shop. They would know someone who knew someone. Maybe they even knew him personally.

But no. I thought I could just waltz in here like the old days. Like nothing had changed. Like he'd still be waiting.

Stupid.

I exhaled shakily, forcing myself to meet Wendy's gaze. "I guess we either leave... or find out for ourselves."

Her brown eyes searched my face, softening as she took a shaky breath.

"What do you want to do?" She whispered. "I'm okay with whatever you decide... but, just so you know, I'm not going down any dark corridors."

A shaky laugh escaped me despite everything. "Fair enough."

I reached for the 'open' button and pressed it with more force than necessary. "Hold the door for me, then."

Wendy's fingers slipped over mine, taking over.

With the torchlight from my phone cutting through the dimness, I wandered down the long corridor. Most of the doors lining the walls were shut tight, though a few stood slightly ajar, their dark gaps hinting at a world I wasn't sure I wanted to see.

With every step, I braced myself for the worst—the creak of a door opening, a figure lunging out to grab me. A small, irrational part of me worried that something far worse—something not human—might slip through the cracks. If a ghost decided to chase me, Wendy would probably save herself and leave me behind. And honestly, I wouldn't blame her.

I shook off the thought and pressed forward, the sound of my footsteps muffled by years of dust and neglect. The air was thick and stale, carrying a faint metallic tang that clung to the back of my throat. At the end of the hallway, just as I was about to turn back, something unexpected cut through the silence.

Music.

I froze. My heart thudding hard against my ribs.

"Can you hear that?" I shouted over my shoulder.

Wendy shouted something back, but her words were distorted. I strained my ears, focusing on the faint melody drifting through the corridor—unmistakably familiar.

Beyond.

It was one of Dannie's favorite bands. I could still remember teasing him about their name sounding like Beyonce. He didn't find it funny. Instead, he'd launched into a passionate explanation about the band's legacy—the tragic death of their lead singer and how the group fell apart afterward. That sadness, he said, made their music unforgettable.

My pulse quickened. He was here. He had to be.

I turned and hurried back toward Wendy. My footsteps echoing through the corridor as fragments of memories tangled with the music in my head.

"He's here," I announced, stepping back into the lift.

Her eyes narrowed. "How do you know?"

"I can hear his music," I pointed toward the darkness, my finger trembling slightly. "But he's obviously changed the password."

Wendy's expression shifted—half curiosity, half exasperation. She tilted her head, one brow arching in that familiar, playful way.

"I always wanted to say this..." She let the words hang for dramatic effect, her smile quirking at the edges.

I sighed, already regretting asking for her help.

"You better have a good idea," I warned, pausing long enough to let my voice drop into a low, serious tone. "A fucking great one."

"Try your birthday."

I shook my head. "It wouldn't work."

"What wouldn't work?"

"My birthday—September fifth." I punched 9, then 5 on the panel.

"Wait, try it the other way around."

"Why?"

"Aren't they ruled by the British or Australia? Just try it the other way!"

I let out a sigh and started over, pressing the number

5, followed by 9. "And 1993, you need three number combinations to—"

The elevator lurched upward, cutting me off

Wendy smirked, her earlier nerves now replaced by a playful confidence. "You were saying?"

She winked at me, as if she'd just cracked the greatest mystery on Earth.

Two seconds later, the doors slid open, revealing a striking contrast to the eerie corridor below. Gone were the dark and grimy corridors. In there place stood a sleek, modern apartment that radiated warmth and elegance.

The ambient lighting, cleverly placed along the ceiling and walls, cast a soft golden hue, making the room feel cozy—homely even. It still amazed me how much thought had gone into the design. Every detail screamed understated luxury. I'd always admired what Dannie's interior designer had done with the place, blending contemporary minimalism with just the right touch of comfort.

Dannie, however, was nowhere to be seen.

We stepped cautiously out of the elevator and into the medium-sized living room. The music—loud and unmistakably Beyond—pulsed through the space, pouring out of the sleek, transparent speaker next to the entertainment unit. The surround sound system I remembered from years ago still lined the room, though he wasn't using it. This felt... casual. As if he hadn't expected company.

I called out three tentative "hellos," each one louder than the last, but only the music answered back.

"Stay here," I instructed Wendy, pointed to the brown

leather three-seater sofa facing the entertainment system. The last thing I needed was for her to go snooping around and stumble into something she shouldn't.

Because this wasn't just anyone's apartment. This was Dannie Wu's apartment.

And he wasn't just anyone.

He was the head of the most successful triad in Hong Kong.

The living room was deliberately separated from the rest of the apartment—a design choice that wasn't about aesthetics. It was practical. This was where Dannie held meetings, and only his most trusted members were ever invited past this point. No one else got a glimpse of what lay beyond the heavy wooden door that divided the space.

I knocked softly on the door, hesitating for a moment before a faint, muffled "Come in" drifted through from the other side.

I pushed it open and stepped inside.

Dannie stood at the kitchen counter, his large hands working a mound of dough. The sight was oddly domestic.

"Hey, you. Long time no see," he said, his voice loud—but the music was louder.

His brow furrowed ever so slightly in irritation before he turned toward the smart speaker. One sharp command later, the blaring sound of Beyond softened to a gentle hum, giving my ears a much-needed break.

The frown on his face faded, and a grin stretched across his lips. It was the same smile I remembered—charming, disarming—but now there were faint wrinkles at the corners of his eyes that hadn't been there before.

"Have a seat," he said, his tone casual. "I'm almost done."

Slowly, I pulled out one of the six chairs at the dining table and lowered myself onto it. This table was new. He used to have a sleek, rectangular glass one—cold, sharp-edges, like him. Now, it had been replaced by a round white marble table, complete with a built-in lazy Susan. It felt... softer. More intimate.

I ran my fingers along the smooth surface before glancing back at him. "What happened to the old table?"

Dannie paused mid-knead, his lips twitching as if debating how much to reveal. "Hmm..." A slight pause. "Someone fell on it."

"Oh." I regretted asking immediately.

The way he said it—calm, flippant—hinted that there was a longer, far more interesting story behind those words. But I wasn't sure I wanted to know who fell on it, or how.

With Dannie, the answer was rarely as simple as it seemed.

"Did you hurt yourself?"

Damn it. I couldn't believe that was the first thing out of my mouth. I didn't care who had destroyed the old table—but I cared about something else. Something that had everything to do with why I was here.

Dannie shook his head, a small smile tugging at his lips. How could someone who smiled like that—soft, boyish, the kind of smile that wouldn't be out of place on a K-pop idol—be so dangerous? I guess that's why people say looks can be deceiving.

I shifted my gaze around the kitchen, noticing it had undergone a makeover too. The once dark wooded cabinets had been replaced by sleek, modern designs—white cupboards with a glossy black countertop. Soft lighting glowed from beneath the upper cabinets, casting a warm brightness over the otherwise windowless space. Everything about it was cleaner, sharper... colder.

"I didn't know you cooked," I said, the words tumbling out before I could stop them. Smooth June.

What else was I supposed to say to my ex while trying to work up the nerve to ask him for a fake document—so I could chase after a man who wasn't even officially my boyfriend?

"I don't, really," he admitted with a small shrug. "But baking calms my nerves."

The irony wasn't lost on me. Given his line of work, I could imagine how much he needed to be calm. Lives depended on him—just like they did on me, though in a very different way.

"Are you any good at it?"

Dannie's smile faded.

"Cut the bullshit, June." His voice hardened, sharp and direct. So much for baking being relaxing. "What do you want from me? Why are you running around Hong Kong like this, looking for a fake visa?"

"I..." The words stuck in my throat. Kai. His face flashed through my mind—a reminder of why I was here.

"How did you know I was here?" I asked, my voice quieter but no less urgent.

Dannie leaned against the counter, arms crossed.

"How could I not know?" His jaw tightened. "I've been looking for Mackie. And thanks to him, I found you."

I froze. Mackie. Or Mackie D—that's what Dannie always called him. My breath hitched.

"You mean... you didn't send him?"

Dannie's eyes darked. "Send him to you? No. Why would I?"

I paused, trying to collect my thoughts.

"I thought you..." I stopped myself. I couldn't bring up the past—not now. I thought he finally wanted revenge for what I did to him, but it was best to leave that wound closed. "Never mind. So... you had me followed?"

His answer was enough to ease one fear—that he had nothing to do with Kai's disappearance.

"No..." He cut the log-shaped dough into even round disks, placing them carefully onto a baking tray lined with parchment paper. "Yes. When my guy spotted you, I told them to keep an eye on you."

I watched his hands—steady, precise—as he lined each disk in perfect rows before sliding the tray into the oven underneath the countertop.

My stomach twisted. How could I not have known? All day people had been following me. Stalking me. Watching my every move. And not just one person— multiple people—with their own motives, their own agendas.

"Then why didn't you help me?"

"With the fake document?" He shut the oven door with a quiet thud.

"Yes."

He grabbed a cloth, wiping down the surface before moving to the sink to wash his hands under the stream of water.

When he finally spoke, his voice was maddeningly casual.

Help you and miss out on the opportunity to see you?" He turned his head slightly, a teasing glint in his eyes. "Now why would I do that?"

A sharp pressure coiled in my chest. Nothing had changed—always the same games.

"How did you know I'd come to you?"

"I didn't." He flicked off the faucet and shook the water from his fingers before filling the kettle. "But here you are."

I shallowed hard, forcing myself to focus on his words and not the way his muscles flexed beneath his shirt.

"Dannie—"

"June."

The way he said my name—smooth, familiar—made my heart skip a beat.

"Don't do that."

"Don't do what?"

"Don't say my name like that," I half-whispered, half-grunted.

"Like what?" He let out a low chuckle. "I don't know what you're talking about."

"Like I'm..." The words tangled in my throat. How could I explain this to him? All I knew was that when he said my name like that, it stripped away my defenses. It made me feel small—like a little woman who needed attention, protection... love. I hated how easily he could do that.

"A puppy or something." I finally blurted out. It wasn't quite right, but it was the closest thing I could come up with.

"I see. But isn't that a good thing? Puppies are cute. People like puppies."

"No one wants to be treated like a puppy, Dannie."

His smile deepened, though his eyes held something darker beneath the surface. "I don't get it. So... that's a bad thing then?"

Our eyes locked. I forced myself to look away, focusing instead on the sleek lines of the remodeled kitchen. "The kitchen's new too. What happened to the old one?"

"Bad people."

His tone was casual—too casual. But I knew I shouldn't have asked. Of course, bad people had done it. In his world, there was no shortage of enemies—the rival gangs, the police, the traitors within his own ranks. And those he'd wrong... or those who simply believed he had.

I swallowed hard, pushing past the unease crawling up my spine. "And the rest of the apartment?"

"They didn't get that far."

Dannie rolled up the sleeves of his sky-blue shirt— left first, then right. But my breath caught when I saw it. A jagged scar stretched across his left arm, cutting through the hawk tattoo I used to trace my fingers over—the one I had always adored.

Without thinking, I reached for his arm, leaping out from the black leather chair too quickly. My foot caught on the edge of the rug, and before I knew it, I was falling. Instinct kicked in—I threw my arms up to shield my face from the inevitable impact. But the floor never came.

Strong hands caught me just in time, pulling me against his chest. One arm wrapped around my waist, steadying me as my heart hammered in my ears.

"Are you okay?" We spoke in unison.

I let out an awkward laugh, brushing off the embarrassment "I'm okay."

"Be careful."

But I wasn't thinking about my fall—I was still thinking about his arm.

"What happened to your arm?" I asked as he helped me to stand upright, his touch warm against my skin.

"You really want to know?"

"Yes." My voice was barely above a whisper, but it felt loud in the quiet tension hanging between us. Part of me had already guessed—a moment of violence—but I needed to hear it from him.

He exhaled slowly. "Cooking incident."

"Really?" It wasn't the answer I expected.

"Yes." His reply was clipped, staccato. He was lying.

"I want to know." I pressed on.

"I told you." His reply slower now, but firm and final.

"I want to know," I repeated, my heart thudding against my ribs. Once, he had told me everything—well, almost everything. He always left out the ugliest details, the ones he thought I couldn't handle.

"No, you can't know everything."

"Why not?"

I wanted us to go back—to the way things used to be.

Even though part of me knew it was impossible. But being here, standing so close to him, I still felt safe. And that much hadn't changed. Not at all.

"That's life. Deal with it."

"Fine."

Rage simmered beneath my skin. I heard it in my own voice. It wasn't fair—I knew that. But I couldn't stop it. The fear, the frustration, the gnawing ache of losing Kai again—it all boiled over, and Dannie was the one standing in the blast zone. He didn't deserve it. He had nothing to do with Kai's disappearance. I repeated that to myself, trying to shove the anger down.

"Don't you 'fine' me," he snapped, his voice like a whip cracking through the air. "I want to know everything too."

"Like what?"

"Like what? I can't believe you have the nerve to ask." His hands curled into fists at his sides, knuckles whitening as the dam finally broke. "First of all—why did you leave without saying goodbye? Do you have any idea how humiliating it was every time someone asked me where the fuck my wife was?"

His voice rose with each word, raw and filled with years of bottled-up anger. "People talked behind my back —laughing at me. 'The boss of the Red Hawk Clan can't even keep his woman.' Do you know what that felt like? Huh? Go ahead—laugh with them."

I didn't laugh.

"And why are you really here, June?" His words hung heavy in the air, vibrating with all the pain I had left behind.

7

____

Kai

Her hair smelled heavenly. I pulled her closer, holding her tighter against me.

Spooning had never been my thing, it was something I used to think was a waste of time. But with June, it felt different. I could've stayed like that forever—just lying there, holding her. I didn't even need to see her face to know how beautiful she looked. There was a warmth in having her in my arms, a sense of calm I hadn't felt in years. She was like a safety blanket—the kind of comfort every kid needs growing up. Her skin was impossibly soft, her curves fitting perfectly against me.

She whispered softly to me. "You are..."

A sudden thud against my back yanked me out of the moment.

Everything blurred. My perfect 20/20 vision faltered, replaced by a hazy mess. The sounds around me faded, swallowed by a sharp ringing buzz in my ears. It wasn't until I felt myself being lifted off the floor that I realized what was happening. The pounding I'd felt—someone's hand on my shoulder.

Trevon.

My best friend from college. What the hell was he doing here?

"We need to go."

We need to go. Those words. Everyone kept saying them to me.

Mario had said them earlier—over and over. My mind scrambled to catch up. Had I blacked out again? With my eyes open? It hadn't happened in years.

I spotted her—Jenny. Blood stained her clothes, her hands, everything. She was hunched over her husband's lifeless body, silent tears streaking down her face.

"Qing," I called out, forcing the words through my brain fog. "We need to go."

Trevon's grip tightened—one of my arms now pinned beneath his broad, dark hands. His voice was low but urgent.

"The police are on their way here. We really have to go."

Jenny shook her head stubbornly. "I should stay. This is all my fault."

I shrugged out of Trevon's grip and crouched down beside my devastated cousin. Her face was pale, streaked with tears, her hands trembling as they clung to her husband's bloodied shirt.

"This is not your fault," I said softly. "You should've never married him. I should've stopped you. You were a victim of your family's politics."

As the words left my mouth, the truth settled heavily on my chest—I wasn't just talking about her. I had been a victim too, trapped and controlled by the same ruthless machine. And worse, I had let them do it.

Jenny's eyes flashed with defiance.

"But we are different," she snapped. "I did love him. He's the father my children, and I still love him—"

"Despite everything…"

"Yes!" She cut me off sharply. "None of this would've happened if I had just played along with his sick game."

At least she knew it was sick.

Trevon crouched beside us. "Why don't we get out of here for now? You'll think more clearly once you've had a chance to breathe."

"He's right." I murmured, running my fingers gently through Jenny's matted hair—the same hair she spent hours and thousands of dollars every month perfecting. "Honey, have you seen Lucy? We need to take her with us."

The realization hit me hard—I hadn't seen Lucy since I arrived.

Jenny's face twisted in confusion as she shook her head. "I don't know. She left in a different car at the airport."

Dread slithered over me. "Is she safe?"

"What?" Her frown told me—she couldn't even process the question, too shattered by grief and guilt.

"Shit. Shit. Shit."

I caught Trevon's gaze, and he didn't look away. I knew the same terrifying thought raced through both our minds.

I turned to Mario, my voice sharp and urgent. "Find Lucy."

"Go, Kai." Jenny demanded, her voice trembling but final. "I'll handle the police when they get here."

"But Qing..."

"I love you, Kai," she spoke over me, "you're the only one in this family who cares about me—the only one I care about. I won't let anything happen to you."

"No, Qing, I—"

"You can't help me if you're locked up too," she insisted, her tone sharper now.

"Come on." Trevon added, he tugged me toward the staircase, pulling me away from Jenny.

"Go!" Jenny screamed, desperation cracking her voice. "I'm begging you!"

Trevon half-dragged my unwilling body down the stairs. My thoughts were a blur, torn between leaving and staying.

As we reached for the massive wooden door—the main entrance and our only exit—a sharp, angry shout pierced the air behind us.

I turned and saw a familiar figure—Chen's head of security. The man was a brute, built like a tank, and had been with Chen longer than anyone else. Unlike the revolving door of bodyguards who never lasted more than two years, he had somehow survived Chen's paranoia and cruelty.

The man spat out a vicious threat in Shanghai dialect —if we took another step, he'd kill the woman in white.

Before I could react, Trevon raised his gun and fired.

The shot echoed through the marble-floored hallway.

The security guard dropped like a stone, his heavy body hitting the ground with a sickening thud.

"What the fuck Trev?" I couldn't believe it—Trevon, the calm, level-headed guy I had known forever had just shot someone without hesitation.

"Relax, it's just an air gun," Trevon said casually.

"But... you just killed him." My voice shaky, as confused as my mind.

We rushed to the fallen fat man. There was no blood, no bullet wound—nothing. Trevon bent down to help the woman to her feet while I checked for a pulse, pressing my fingers against the thick skin of his neck.

Living and breathing.

He had fainted—somehow. Good luck to Chen if he decided to keep him around.

A distant, eerie howling broke through the tense silence. I swallowed hard, guilt gnawing at me. It was too much for Jenny to face all this alone.

As if Trevon had read my mine—he shook his head sharply, silently telling me to keep moving.

As we rose to leave, the woman we helped earlier grabbed my hand, her grip surprisingly strong. Without a word, she led us through the mansion's dim corridors to a discreet back door.

Outside, she pressed a Buick key into my palm and pointed at a blue car parked among a row of beaten-up vehicles.

"Take the unkempt path behind the house—follow it until you're clear." She whispered in rapid Mandarin.

Before I could thank her, she shoved us out the door and locked it behind us.

We followed her instructions, the Buick's engine rumbling as we crept along the overgrown path. At first, it felt like we were going in circles—twisting and turning deeper into the estate's sprawling grounds. But after a few agonizing minutes, we reached a narrow wooden gate, just wide enough for the car to squeeze through.

On the other side was a hidden road, winding along the backside of the mountain. A perfect escape route.

In the distance, the shrill wail of police sirens pierced the night.

My chest tightened as I thought of Jenny. At least she's safe—for now.

"Whose car is this?" Trevon finally asked, though we both knew I didn't have an answer.

"Don't know. But we should ditch this car as soon as we get the chance."

Trevon gripped the wheel, driving like he knew exactly where he was going. In reality, there were only two choices—up or down the mountain. He chose down, leaving the estate and its dark secrets behind us.

"I have some news for you." Trevon announced, his tone sharp and urgent.

I froze, heart pounding in my chest, and gave him a quick nod to continue.

"June and Wendy are on their way to Hong Kong. We should head there as soon as possible."

"June? Lincoln's sister?" My stomach twisted in disbelief. "But why?"

"To look for you, you idiot," he snapped. "Hong Kong is as far as she could go without a visa for China."

"I..." Words failed me. My thoughts felt tangled and

disjointed. I hadn't even had a chance to process the chaos of my day—or days. How long had it been since I left the United States? Everything had happened so fast. It was all a blur. My fingers instinctively reached for my phone in my pocket— but came up empty.

"You left without a word. No one knew where the fuck you went. June thought you'd been taken and flew out to find you." Trevon said, his voice low but edged with frustration.

"She did?" The thought made my pulse jump. I shifted on my feet, a nervous energy buzzing through me —like a schoolboy hearing the news about his favorite girl.

"Yes. She showed up at Lincoln's in the middle of night, begging him to fly her to you on his private jet," he said, shaking his head in disbelief.

"No, shit." Guilt gnawed at me. I had left without words—without a single explanation. I needed to call her. "I should call her."

My hands darted to my pockets—shirt, jacket— frantic now. "Damn it. Mario smashed my phone at the house."

"Wait! Don't tell me your phone is at the crime scene?"

"Fuck." The weight of it hit me like a punch to the gut.

Trevon gave me a more detailed update about what had happened with June and Wendy on the way to the airport. Unlike Lincoln and I, he didn't own a private jet, nor was he a member of some exclusive airplane club that could charter him anywhere he wanted to go. He preferred to fly commercial, he said, but we all knew the truth. He didn't want to raise any alarms or attract attention to his financial status. Trevon simply didn't like people knowing how rich he actually was.

The next flight to Hong Kong was in three hours, and Trevon had convinced me that flying commercial might be the better option. For one, it wouldn't look like I was trying to flee the country. Well, flying private wouldn't seem suspicious either, considering how often I did it—but my head wasn't actually functioning today after everything that had happened. I trusted Trevon to have my best interests at heart. He wouldn't do anything to harm me.

Besides, I suspected my mother was already looking for me. Flying private would alert her immediately to my whereabouts, and it wouldn't take her long to track me down in Hong Kong with her resources. Flying commercial, on the other hand, might buy me some time—long enough for her to believe I was still in Shanghai.

I tried to stay aware of my surroundings, scanning for anyone following us. So far, I hadn't noticed anyone suspicious—but it was only a matter of time before someone found me. The fact that no one had yet led me to wonder if I had managed to shake off the two hundred pairs of eyes on my payroll. Still, I knew that wasn't very likely.

Over the years, I'd lost count of how many people my mother and Dave had hired for my security. All I knew was that it never seemed to be enough. And yet, somehow, I didn't feel like anyone was watching, following or protecting us now.

And Trevon? He didn't have security of his own. He didn't believe in it.

"Can they track your phone?" I asked, my voice low.

I frowned as I watched Trevon turn on the navigation app on his phone and type in 'airport'.

"Why would someone track my phone?" he replied, raising an eyebrow.

He had a point. No one expected Trevon to show up like this. He'd never visited me in Shanghai—ever.

"How did you find me so quickly?"

Trevon flicked on the turn signal, making a smooth left as the navigation app suggested.

"I was in Bangkok when Lincoln called. He wanted me to check on the girls, but the last time I spoke to Wendy, they seemed to be doing fine. So, I figured you might need more help than they do. Besides, no one really knew where the fuck you were."

"My phone..." I tried to remember the last time I'd used it before Mario smashed it. If I had to guess, it was when I asked Dave to swear to protect June with his life— just before I flew out of America. After that, Clare had handled the rest of my affairs while we were on the jet.

I lowered the electric window, letting the cool fresh air rush in. The lingering scent of cigarettes was starting to get to me. This must have been the housekeeper's car —but she didn't seem like the type who smoked.

"I messed up," I admitted, the words heavy on my tongue.

"I know," Trevon said, his tone flat.

I rolled my eyes. Seriously? Shouldn't my best friend be on my side during a tough time like this?

"But you are doing your best," he added after a beat. "Honestly, I'm surprised you didn't curl up on the floor and have a panic attack like..."

But I sort of had when he found me.

Something had changed. Sure, I'd had a mini blackout—wide awake but completely numb—but I was handling things better than I would've in the past. Then again, it's not like witnessing a murder right in front of me was an everyday occurrence.

"I shut down..." I confessed quietly.

"I bet." Trevon's voice softened. He'd seen it happen before— back when we were in boarding school. There had been more than a few occasions when I thought someone was coming for me.

"June must think I led her on," I murmured, guilt twisting in my stomach. "Leaving her behind without a word, again."

"It's not your fault. Try to take it easy, bro."

"What is she going to think of me now..." I muttered, the weight of it pressing down on me.

"She thought you were kidnapped, actually."

"What?" I dragged a hand down my face, rubbing hard enough to feel the scrape of my shadow of facial hair—just to ground myself, to be sure I was awake and not trapped in some surreal nightmare. "Why?"

"Well, all three of you went missing, didn't you? Lincoln said she was panicking when he saw her."

"Fuck. I hope Link won't kill me for this."

"Nah, come on. He knows you. He wouldn't have asked me to come for you if he was mad."

"How did you even know where to find me?"

"Wendy gave me Clare's number."

I nodded slowly as the pieces started to click together. Everything made more sense now that Trevon was laying it out. My nerves, still raw, began to settle—if only a little.

"What exactly are their plans in Hong Kong?"

Trevon chuckled under his breath, like something about the whole situation genuinely amused him.

"Well, you remember Wendy?"

"Yes, I remember Wendy," I said, rolling my eyes.

"She knows all kind of people around the world."

"You mean *shady* people?" I raised a brow at him.

He glanced at me, his chuckle deepening. "Yeah, exactly."

"So, what's her plan?"

"Fake ID," Trevon said, flashing a grin.

"You like her..." I teased, watching him carefully.

He didn't answer—but he didn't deny it either.

"Shouldn't we book a flight or something?" I asked, shifting the conversation back to the urgent matter at hand.

"Clare's on it."

That was Trevon—he always had a plan. But sometimes, his plans failed when it came to being a person. He lived his life according to a strict blueprint, and it worked. He'd achieved everything he ever wanted—success in business, a thriving career, and wealth most people only dreamed of. But fun? That was never part of his plan. It took too much time. He used to scoff at us whenever we asked him to relax, to join us for a night out.

When we arrived at the airport, Clare was already

waiting for us. I scanned the area quickly. There was no one else in sight.

"Good to see you again, Sir," she greeted me with an unfamiliar politeness. I couldn't remember the last time she was this formal—maybe during her interview or the first few weeks on the job. It had been a while.

Trevon tossed her the car keys without a word, a clear signal to get rid of the vehicle. Clare caught them effortlessly and handed them off to a middle-aged woman who appeared silently from behind her. I had been wrong—she did bring backup.

I strode into the airport, pausing in front of a towering row of flight information screens.

"It's gate 59, Sir," Clare said smoothly, already anticipating my question.

Trevon's tall frame was easy to spot at a ticket desk. In a sea of faces, he stood out—not just because he was the only Black man around, but because he had a presence no one could ignore. When he turned and caught my eye, he waved, holding what I hoped were our tickets.

"My guy could only get us business class seats," Trevon said as he handed me mine. "First class was completely sold out"

"Thanks. It sounds like you had some help getting these?"

"It's a full flight, but my friend made it work. She offered her clients a ridiculous amount of air miles and bumped them to first class if they agreed to fly later."

"Win-win," I muttered.

Without wasting another second, we headed toward

security. I didn't need to turn around to know that familiar, unwanted presence was still trailing us.

I stopped abruptly and snapped. "Where do you think you're going."

"I need to protect you, Sir."

Her voice was steady, but it was the reflection of the harsh airport lighting that gave her away. Without it, I might have missed the shimmer of her watery blue eyes —bright and unyielding as they locked onto mine.

"Haven't you done enough?" I shook my head, frustration curling in my gut. This mess—part of it—was my fault. I'd let her get too comfortable, too relaxed with her job. If I had drawn the line earlier—stopped her from joking around, from bossing Dave and others who were far more experienced—maybe things wouldn't have spiraled out of control. I knew the moment I hired her that she was young and arrogant. I just thought time would change that. If only I had given her a real chance to learn.

"Let me make it up to you," she pleaded.

"I have Mario." Though, in truth, I wouldn't trust him with my life. He wasn't trained security, just a thug willing to do anything for the right price.

"Please, Sir, Mr. Li." Her voice trembled as she swallowed hard. "I made a mistake... and I don't know how you could ever forgive me."

Before I could respond, she dropped to her knees. I froze in disbelief as she lowered herself further, about to perform a kowtow—an ancient gesture of apology.

"Get up. Get up!" I hissed through clenched teeth.

But of course, the stubborn woman refused to move.

"I'll kneel here until you forgive me," she said, her tone unwavering.

I sighed, knowing she wouldn't stay there forever. Airport security would have her up and out in five minutes if she kept this up.

"You're fucking embarrassing me," I muttered under my breath, my voice low enough for only her to hear.

People were already staring. I could feel their judgmental eyes burning into me—painting me as some heartless asshole who bullied women. And God, I hated that feeling. I was a lot of things, but I had never bullied a woman in my life.

"Get up," I sighed, exasperation dripping from my words. "How are you going to get a ticket if you're still on the floor?"

8

____

June

I opened my mouth, then closed it again. I repeated the motion a few times, feeling like a sore loser—a wreck, a coward.

Dannie stood there, arms crossed over his chest, waiting for an answer. His gaze pinned me in place, patient but expectant.

What was I really here for?

The simple answer was for a fake document—something, anything that would allow me to enter to China. That's what I thought, at least until I saw his scar. Now, I wanted to know more.

His sleeves were rolled up, exposing the length of the jagged scar. A large, rough line stretched vertically down his arm—an ugly, raised caterpillar. The stitches were clumsy, and uneven. Someone inexperienced had done it —and they'd done it in a hurry.

I shouldn't have cared. But when he held me up

earlier, I felt an irrational urge to fall into his arms—to sink into the familiar warmth of his embrace. The scent of him, clean and sharp with a hint of spice, was intoxicating. It called to me like a siren's song.

"I really do need those travel documents," I said, trying to steady my voice.

He laughed, low and bitter, shaking his head. Not a single strand of his perfectly styled hair moved.

"You know it's illegal, right?"

"Yes, so?" The good girl inside me flinched at the thought of doing something criminal—but what choice did I have? "Are you going to help me or not?"

His jaw tightened.

"Who is he? The guy you're so desperate to see?" He turned back to the oven, brushing off the question like it didn't matter—but I knew it did.

"He's a friend," I said, though even to my own ears, it didn't sound convincing.

The moment he opened the oven door, the rich, buttery scent of cookies flooded the room. My stomach growled in response—either the cookies were incredible, or I was hungrier than I realized.

"Don't lie to me." He dropped the baking tray onto the counter with a loud clang. "I know Kai Li is rich, but he wouldn't go above and beyond to impress a girl at a gala. What did he pay for a handful of dates?"

"How did you know that?"

"My guy, remember?"

I nodded. Of course. Ever since Kai entered my life, I'd been exposed to all kinds of surveillance and stalking. Privacy? That was a distant memory.

"That's none of your business."

"Well," he drawled, his voice tight and dry.

"If only I knew you could be bought with money…" He cleared his throat with a rough cough before continuing, "I could've easily paid you that ten years ago."

His words struck like a slap. I picked up my phone, staring blankly at the screen, willing myself to come up with a venomous comeback. But nothing came. A few messages from Link flashed across the display, but now wasn't the time to deal with him.

"The money was for charity," I said, hating the defensiveness in my tone.

"How noble of you." His sarcasm cut deep. "You must really care about that charity of yours. So much so that you fucked him right there as a token of appreciation, huh?"

His face flushed an angry shade of tomato red, and the vein at his temple budged with tension.

"How could you spy on me like that?"

He let out a bitter laugh. "Why do it in public if you didn't want anyone to see?"

I paced back and forth across his kitchen, my heartbeat thudding in my ears.

"I think I even have a video," he added, pulling his phone from his pocket and waving it at me. A triumphant, twisted smile spread across his face.

"You're disgusting," I spat, my stomach in knots.

"Who is disgusting? Me?" He raised a brow, his tone mockingly innocent.

Tears blurred my vision and spilled down my cheeks before I could stop them. I didn't know what hurt more—

the fact that he had spied on me, or that he owned a copy of what I had done. Maybe they were the same thing.

I did like him. And judging by the ache in my chest, I still did—at least, part of me. But it burned knowing that he had witnessed the wildest, rawest side of me. I wasn't the perfect, innocent girl he had once dated.

"Hey, hey, hey..." He closed the space between us. Before I could react, I was wrapped in his arms again. "You want a cookie? They're really nice."

"They do smell lovely."

Just like that, I was no longer in his arms. Instead, I found myself sitting at his sleek new marble table, a plate of cookies placed in front of me as if nothing had happened. Classic Dannie—disarming me with a small gestures while keeping his true intentions hidden.

"Listen, June, I didn't mean to do all that to you."

"Oh yeah?" Without hesitation, I grabbed a cookie and took a big bite. For all I knew, they could be poisoned —but that didn't seem like his style.

No, Dannie liked to be up close. He preferred to feel the life drain from his enemies, to watch them struggle for air and choke on their own saliva. The memory of him explaining why it was more "honorable" than poison sent a shiver down my spine.

"Lavender?" I asked, trying to identify the delicate floral note lingering on my tongue.

"Yes," he confirmed, leaning back casually. "What else can you taste?"

I chewed slowly, trying to place the underlying sweet- ness. "Hmm... dates?"

The flavor was rich and complex, nothing like the

artificial sugar rush of store-bought cookies. "Did you use some kind of sweetener?"

"No sugar. Just monk fruit."

"Right." I nodded, more to myself. "I've heard of monk fruit sweetener before, but I didn't know you could bake with it."

And just like that, we fell into an easy rhythm—chit-chatting as if the last ten seconds of anger, of accusations, had never happened. That was the thing about Dannie. He always knew how to smooth over the rough edges, how to make me forget my troubles—even when he was one of them.

"When you left…" he slid his hand over mine, warm and steady. With his other hand, he offered me another cookie. "I was worried. Then I was angry. Not at you—at myself. I kept wondering what I did wrong."

"You weren't mad at me?" I asked, my words softer than I intended.

"Not at first." His lips curled into a crooked smile— the kind that always made me weak in the knees.

"It was understandable if you were angry. I was angry at myself for a long time." For getting into a marriage that became more real than I ever intended. For leaving him behind without a word.

And suddenly, I understood—when Kai left me, it wasn't just him I was mad at. I was angry at myself. Karma really did come full circle.

"Everywhere I went, people kept asking where my wife was," he said. "At first, I made up lies. Then I just… stopped talking about you altogether."

"And you never saw anyone after that?" I asked, trying to sound casual, though my pulse quickened.

"I did. I had to."

"You *had* to?" I raised a brow. "Someone holding a gun to your head?"

He smirked but didn't laugh.

"One—to stop people from asking about my wife, thanks to you. Two—to shut down the rumors that I was gay. And," his voice dipped lower, rougher, "I have needs."

I cleared my throat, willing my expression to stay neutral. "At least you're honest."

He leaned back against the chair, studying me like he was trying to figure out how much of this I could take. "What kind of lies did you tell people about me?"

He shook his head. "Nothing bad."

"I don't believe you." I pulled my hand from under his and started dismantling the cookie he gave me, breaking it apart piece by piece. "What did you tell them? And what did they say about... us?"

His lips curved into a smile—gentle, unguarded. The kind only a few people ever got to see. And once, I'd been one of those people.

"I would never talk bad about you. Ever." There was something else beneath his words. "But... I did tell a few harmless silly lies. Really silly ones."

"Tell me." I nudged, curiosity winning over pride.

He watched me for a beat longer before giving in. "At first, I told people you were in Paris on a shopping trip."

I laughed softly, shaking my head. "Not the worst excuse. I wouldn't mind a romantic getaway to Paris."

"Yeah, well, that backfired fast," he admitted, running

a hand through his hair. "Everyone wanted to know why I wasn't with you. Paris is a honeymoon destination, after all. According to them, I was a terrible husband for not tagging along."

"They had a point." I popped a piece of a cookie in my mouth, savoring the sweetness. "So...what did you say to that?"

"Business, of course. No one dares ask another questions when a triad boss says he has *business* to deal handle." He air-quoted the second 'business' with a smirk.

It would be foolish to think people hadn't gossiped about us. People gossip. In Hong Kong, entire magazines were dedicated to exposing every scandal. Who was dating who? Who was screwing who? Who was climbing the social ladder—by any means necessary? I wasn't sure if I wanted to know what they said about me. People could be cruel.

"S'pose," I murmured, my fingers tracing the edge of the cookies. "Where else did I go?"

Though I'd earned enough as a doctor to retire early, I had never really traveled. Work trips, yes—but never leisure. Not since Hong Kong.

"Singapore. China. Back to the US to finish your studies. Then... I stopped talking about you..." His voice dipped at the end, like the words carried a weight even he hadn't fully let go of.

"Funny you mentioned China—I didn't actually have a visa to go there."

"About that," he said easily. "I know someone in the embassy. They could fast-track your visa if you wanted."

"Really?" The half-eaten cookie slipped from my fingers, landing on the table. "Oh my God, I can't believe this!"

Without thinking, I lunged at him, wrapping my arms around his neck.

His chest rumbled with a quiet laughter as his arms closed around me. For a moment, nothing else mattered.

"Hello."

The voice sliced through the warmth like a blade.

Before I could process it, Dannie had pulled a gun from the back of his waistband. In a single, fluid movement, he twisted me onto his lap and aimed the weapon at Wendy.

"Fuck," I screamed.

"Put the gun down," Wendy said calmly, raising her hands in the air.

I should've done something—said something—but I was frozen. My mind spun, struggling to catch up with the rapid turn of events.

I wasn't sure what shocked me more.

Wendy barging in unannounced.

Dannie pulling a gun on her like it was nothing.

Or the fact that, straddling his lap, I could feel the hard, unmistakable bulge beneath me.

God help me—I didn't want to move.

"No one comes in here," Dannie said, his tone low and dangerous. He slid a glance sideways at me, his grip on the gun unwavering. "Except you, of course."

The way Wendy barged in stirred an old memory—a young guy, cocky and reckless, bursting through the door. He had interrupted the first kiss Dannie and I shared, our first taste of something deeper. I remembered how fast it happened—Dannie lifting him by the throat, pinning him against the wall like he weighed nothing, before throwing him to the floor. If his friends hadn't arrived, that guy wouldn't have walked out of there in one piece.

"She's a friend!" I screamed, though our faces were only inches apart.

"She's not a friend to me," he murmured, his face unreadable. His finger twitched against the trigger. "Do you know what's happened in this room?"

I swallowed hard and dipped my head slightly. I knew too well.

Once, this floor had been open—anyone in his triad with a password could reach the top. And they did. Attack after attack. Betrayal after betrayal. Until he locked it down—only senior members had access now. But even that wasn't foolproof. When the people closest to you turned, the wounds cut deeper.

Could I blame him for trusting no one?

No, I couldn't.

And maybe that's why I couldn't blame him for pointing a gun at Wendy either.

"It's just instinct," I reminded myself. But that didn't stop the cold sweat trailing down my back.

"But she's my friend," I said again—softer this time. Almost pleading.

Dannie's lips curled into something cruel.

"Your friend, honey?" The words dripped with doubt.

"Yes. I trust my life with her." I met his gaze, steady and unyielding.

Trust.

It meant very little to Dannie.

But not to me. I needed him to know that.

"So... she won't hurt you?"

I shook my head slowly from side to side.

"I see."

Dannie lowered his gun. The breath I didn't realize I was holding rushed out of me as I stepped toward Wendy.

"Hi, nice to meet you. Dannie Wu. Not Daniel—the gorgeous movie star. Dannie—the badass triad boss. That's me." His voice was smooth, playful, like he hadn't just been a heartbeat away from pulling the trigger.

Wendy's eyes flicked between us, her usual confidence faltering.

"Right... nice to meet you. Not the movie star Dannie Wu." Her voice wavered, words broken as if her brain struggled to catch up with her mouth. Then, as if remembering herself, she threw out something that made my jaw drop. "It kind of defeats the point of being a badass when you actually have to say the word *badass*."

Dannie's lips curled into an amused smirk. "Noted."

And just like that, he turned on the charm—flipping the switch with unnerving ease.

"Cookies?" He lifted the tray toward her, his tone warm and inviting.

"I want to say no, but..." Wendy hesitated for only a second before grabbing one with her slightly trembling fingers. "They smell too good to resist."

I scanned her face. "Are you okay?"

No matter how tough Wendy was, having a loaded

gun pointed at you—especially by *him*—wasn't something you shook off easily.

She shrugged off my concern with a casualness I wasn't sure I believed.

"These cookies are amazing. Tastes like something you'd buy at a fancy store." She took another bite.

"Really?" Dannie's smile shifted. This one touched his eyes, warming the edges of his otherwise cold, mysterious gaze.

"Yes, like the kind you find in those boutique bakeries. Expensive. Exclusive. You know?"

"Glad you approve," he extended the tray again. "Take another."

It wasn't a suggestion—it was a quiet command.

Wendy arched a brow, hesitating just long enough to test his patience before snatching another cookie. "Thanks."

Dannie's expression softened further—danger still lingering beneath the surface. "I heard what you did for June. Thank you for looking after her. You have no idea how much I appreciate that."

Wendy tilted her head, curiosity flickering across her face. "Oh, that? It was nothing. I'm always happy to help a friend."

"You'll be handsomely rewarded."

Dannie extended his right hand toward Wendy.

Without hesitation, she shook it.

"What are you doing?" I asked, though I wasn't sure who the question was directed at.

"We don't need Wendy now, honey. You've got me." Dannie explained. His jaw tightened, but the corner of his mouth curved upward, betraying the game he was playing.

I frowned, crossing my arms over my chest. I wasn't stupid. Whatever this was, it was about control. Maybe when we were catching up earlier, he'd been genuine. But now? I was certain he had a plan, and I was at the center of it.

"What are you doing?" I repeated, my voice louder, sharper.

Dannie's smile deepened. "I heard you the first time, sweetheart. But tell me—who's better to look after you than your own husband?"

Husband. The word rolled off his tongue too easily, like a reminder I couldn't escape.

"I need a word with Wendy," I said, forcing myself to stay calm. "Please."

"Honey—"

"*Please.*" I pleaded.

Without another word, Dannie stepped back. His gaze lingered on me before he turned and disappeared through a door opposite the one Wendy had barged through.

Behind that door lay the rest of his fortress—a penthouse, a sky mansion, or whatever you called a space carved out of twenty abandoned apartments. Kam Sha was the most haunted building in Hong Kong, and its former residents had been desperate to leave. They sold their home for far less than they were worth, preferring to escape whatever ghost stories clung to the place.

But to Dannie? A place no one dared to enter was the perfect sanctuary.

"Are you okay?" I asked Wendy again. My voice softer now.

She exhaled a shaky breath. "Shit scared. He's freakishly terrifying."

"Yeah," I admitted, glancing toward the closed door. "I know he can be."

"But he isn't with you."

"We knew each other for a very long time," I paused as the words hung awkwardly between us. The truth was—we didn't really know each other that long. I had met him ten years ago, sure, but the time we actually spent together wasn't very long. "We had some kind of..."

"Connection," Wendy supplied.

"What? No—I mean, understanding."

"Yeah. Right."

I wasn't naive. Whatever this was—whatever he was doing—Dannie wouldn't let the past slide. I had left him after our so-called wedding, walking away and leaving him to deal with the aftermath. In my defense, it was supposed to be a fake ceremony—to fulfill the wish of his dying grandfather.

But even fake vows had consequences.

"I'm sorry he pulled a gun on you."

My fingers brushed against my neck—a nervous reflex. I couldn't shake off the memory of the hot-headed guy who once stormed in here.

"He's in love with you, then."

"This is not the time to joke." I shifted uncomfortably. Just because I left that room unharmed didn't mean I was safe. And now wasn't exactly the time to explain to her that Dannie might very well be plotting a payback for me.

"Whatever," Wendy mocked. "What happened in here? You've been gone for a while."

"Not much," I lied.

"Did he say he'd help you?"

"Yes, he said he knows someone who can get me a visa. Fast."

A laugh—short, sharp—escaped her lips. "So, after all that, the badass triad boss is going to help you get a *legit* travel document?"

"Yes, and don't call him that." I snapped. "He's not a bad person."

Despite everything—despite the blood on his hands—some part of me still wanted to defend him. Maybe because I knew he never did anything without a reason. Even if those reasons were fucked up.

Her lips pressed into a thin flat line. Then, gradually, she relaxed. "Well... don't forget he sent people to hurt you."

"Mack?" I asked. "He's got nothing to do with Mack."

"Oh?"

"Yeah, I asked him." I lifted my chin, sounding more confident that I felt.

My gaze fixed on her face as questions flooded my mind. The men who took Dave—were they connected to Dannie or Mack? Were they there for me instead of Dave? And if Dave hadn't been there, would they have taken me instead?

Was Dannie hiding something?

What was he really after?

"Can you..." I hesitated, glancing around the room as

if cameras might be hidden in the shadows. "Can you stay with me? Don't leave me here alone."

Wendy's fingers curled around my hand, her grip steady. "Of course. Actually... I think I have to."

Her tone was off—quiet, careful. And her eyes, sharp and searching, scanned the room like she expected something.

"What is it? What aren't you telling me?" I swallowed hard.

Dannie leaned against the frame, his smile a dangerous curve. "Are you guys done with your girl talk?"

9

———

June

"Wendy is staying," I announced as Dannie emerged from the other side of the wall. My voice was loud and clear, leaving no room for him to pretend he didn't hear me.

"Great. Then she'll come with us."

Dannie had changed. His perfectly pressed three-piece dark suit hugged his frame a little too tightly, especially across his chest. It left little to the imagination about the toned body underneath.

"Where are we going?" I asked, watching as he slipped on the watch he had left on the dining table. "Can we just check into a hotel or something? We could both use some rest."

Wendy nodded in agreement beside me.

"Oh honey... I'm so sorry you're tired. Can you hang on a little longer?" His voice dripped with saccharine sweetness, the kind that made me feel like he was patronizing a small child. "Grandma is expecting us."

"Grandma?" I echoed, my breath hitching in surprise. "How does she know I'm here?"

I remembered her vividly. When I first met her, she had been nothing but kind—almost too kind. She showered me with gifts and warmth, a level of generosity I never experienced from a stranger. But it wasn't just her kindness that lingered in my memory—there was something else, something unforgettable.

I didn't mind seeing her again. But every detour Dannie planned only pushed me farther from getting to Kai. And I hadn't forgotten about Kai. No matter how much I wanted to reach Kai, I had no choice but to rely on Dannie for now. Unless I found another way, I needed to play along with whatever he had planned.

"I was just on the phone with her," Dannie said, grabbing a container and stuffing it with cookies. "She was so excited that we finally made up."

"You... I..." I opened my mouth but quickly closed it again. He must have told her something about us—he had to explain my disappearance somehow.

"It's her birthday today. What better way to cheer her up than by telling her that you're here?"

I marched to Dannie's side and opened the box he had just filled, frowning at the crushed cookies he had clumsily assembled. I removed the broken pieces and carefully rearranged the rest in a neat order. "Those flowers—can we give them to her? I don't have anything else to bring."

"You want to give Grandma some flowers?"

"Yes."

"That can be arranged." He pulled out his phone, tapped on the screen, and barked a quick command. "Done. She's going to be very happy to see you. Us. Together."

"Your grandad?"

Last time I saw Dannie's grandma was at our wedding. Because of Dannie's unique circumstances, we skipped the traditional door games. Besides, I didn't have any friends who could host them. We did have a tea ceremony where we knelt and served tea to the elders—some were family, others were powerful senior members of the triad. Afterward, we held a dinner reception, which was similar to an American wedding, except I wore a traditional Chinese red and gold wedding dress called a *kua*.

"He passed away a few months after you took off."

"I'm sorry."

His grandad had been dying of cancer. That was the real reason behind the wedding—to fulfill his grandad's dying wish: to see Dannie married.

I never understood why it meant so much to him. Dannie once explained that his grandad had never gotten over his father's horrific murder. His body had been cut up in pieces and fed to stray dogs. His grandma had fainted when the police informed her they had found his father's head inside a soup pot in a holiday home. Dannie's father had been the head of the triad then. With him gone, his grandad was forced out of retirement to take over. Dannie couldn't bear to watch him carry that burden again, so he stepped up and assumed his father's role as the head of triad.

There were many objections and complaints—mostly about how young Dannie was when he took over. But with his grandad's guidance, the older members eventually fell in line. And as the only male in the family, it was crucial that Dannie continue the family name.

How could I say no to that proposal after hearing the whole story? Even though it was all fake, we did it for a good cause.

"He's in a better place now." Dannie's eyes fixed on an ornament a few feet away, his expression distant and thoughtful. "I know people always say that, but it was true for him. The chemo was killing him more than saving him."

"Should I bring something too?" Wendy's soft voice broke the silence. She had a point—she'd been dragged into this situation without much choice. "Maybe we could stop somewhere on the way there?"

"That sounds like a great idea."

I latched onto the suggestion, relieved at the thought of delaying our visit to Dannie's beloved grandma. She had always been kind, but it had been ten years since I last saw her. How she felt about me now might be entirely different from how she felt back then.

Dannie didn't like going to public places. His fear of being attacked at any moment, from any corner, might have seemed paranoid—but it wasn't impossible. This was a man who had been ambushed in his own home, for God's sake. No one could blame him for feeling unsafe in the outside world.

"Fine. Let's make a move. My driver's waiting."

We took the same shabby elevator down the building. As soon as we reached the lobby, a sleek black Toyota minivan pulled up. Dannie waved at the driver inside, slid the door open, and gestured for Wendy to take a seat in the back row.

I climbed in next, settling into one of the two middle-row seats. Dannie followed, taking the seat beside me, and slid the door shut. I had ridden in these luxury minivans before during my time working in Korea and Japan —they were wildly popular in Asia. But as soon as the heavy door clicked shut, the noise from the outside world vanished. The silence was eerie, thicker than in a regular car. That's when I realized—the minivan was bulletproof. The thick, heavy doors and reinforced windows weren't just for show.

The driver, a man in his late forties, turned around and handed Dannie a bouquet before he drove on. Without even glancing at it, Dannie passed it to me. It was a bundle of sunflowers, skillfully wrapped in a mix of white stiff paper and transparent plastic, finished with a yellow ribbon that read 'Happy Day'.

"They're Grandma's favorite," he said.

"Sunflowers? I thought she liked yellow roses?" That was what my memory told me. I didn't recall much from those days, but somehow, that detail stuck with me.

"New favorite," he corrected himself. "She still loves roses—buys them herself sometimes—but she says it's weird receiving yellow roses from anyone other than Grandad."

"That's kind of romantic."

"Yeah. Grandad used to bring her yellow roses every Friday."

"Friday? Why Friday?"

"I never asked."

We pulled up to an upscale grocery store nestled at the base of the mountain where Dannie's grandma lived. As I stepped out of the van, I noticed two black cars trailing behind us. When they stopped, two men emerged—one from each vehicle. Both wore black short-sleeve T-shirts and bore matching eagle tattoos on their right arm. Not quite the same eagle as Dannie's, but close enough to be part of the same world.

Dannie guided Wendy and me inside the store.

"Tell me you saw them," Wendy whispered as we walked side by side, scanning the aisles for something appropriate—a gift fit for a respected ex-triad lady boss.

I hooked my arm around hers and murmured, "Yeah, I saw them."

Dannie wasn't shopping. Instead, he shadowed us, lingering near the ends of the aisles, his presence steady but distant. The two men? Nowhere to be seen—but I knew they were close.

The store wasn't particularly busy. Besides the usual crowd, there was an unusual number of white people mingling among the shelves—an odd ratio for a place like this. I wondered if there was some kind of expat community nearby, but there was no way to know without striking up a conversation.

We considered buying fruit, but it felt too impersonal. Wendy suggested a box of fancy chocolates, but I vetoed the idea. My medical background had taught me that people over seventy often struggled with diabetes, and I didn't want to risk it. After a brief debate, we settled on a bottle of collectible aged Sake. It felt like the perfect choice—something she could drink, keep as family heirloom, or pass along as a thoughtful gift.

We headed to the checkout like any regular customers after deciding to make a purchase. However, Dannie waved at us, signaling for us to leave the store without paying. I couldn't do that. I had never stolen anything in my life, and I wasn't about to start.

I marched straight up to the cashier, my heart pounding in my chest. His eyes flicked from me to Dannie, then back again. Was he too afraid to take my money? I slammed down more than enough cash on the counter and turned on my heel, leaving without another word.

The rest of the journey passed in tense, uncomfortable silence. I hated how much power Dannie seemed to have over people. Even the cashier had been too scared to accept my money. Why did he have to be like this? Did he extort protection money from that store too? I thought his influence only extended to small, old shops like the tart shop Wendy and I had visited earlier.

If Dannie had been at the tart shop, would the sweet couple have refused to take our money too?

Was leaving cash at the cashier the right thing to do? Would the cashier dare to touch it with Dannie looming over him like a shadow? Especially with two scary thugs outside, their tattooed arms crossed menacingly over their chests as they watched us with cold, unyielding eyes.

I glanced down at the bottle of Sake I had taken from the store. Wondering how much trouble I had brought him.

Suddenly, a wave of unease swept over me as I felt the full weight of Dannie's presence. He was intimidating, there was no denying it. But before I could process my emotions, the van rolled to a stop, and the door slid open with a mechanical hiss.

A woman with vibrant purple hair stood waiting, her eyes sharp as they swept over us. Behind her, two lines of people stood opposite each other, side by side, forming a human corridor. Dannie stepped out first, his movements calm and controlled. Without a word, he held his hand out to help me out. I ignored the gesture and motioned for Wendy to go ahead, still mad about what happened at the shop.

Wendy was immediately intercepted by two females who began frisking her with cold efficiency. They patted her, top to bottom, removing her phone from her bag without a hint of apology. When I braced myself for my turn, Dannie waved them off with a dismissive gesture.

"It's just standard procedure," he said to Wendy, his tone unapologetic.

I folded my arms across my chest.

"What about me? Aren't you afraid I might attack you?" I snapped, my voice dripping with sarcasm.

Dannie met my glare for a quick second before looking away. His usual cocky arrogance was still there, but there was something else beneath it, something harder to define.

His grandmother's estate was perched high on

Victoria Peak, a sprawling property with enough land to make any real estate mogul envious. In Hong Kong, land was the ultimate luxury—a status symbol reserved for the unimaginably wealthy. Families who owned such estates rarely let them go, passing them down through generations like prized heirlooms.

Dannie's family, however, hadn't always been rich. But once he took control of the triad, his knack for manipulation and power plays had propelled them to unimaginable wealth. Within a few years, he had outshone his father and secured this mansion, ensuring his family's legacy in one of the most prestigious locations in the city.

I didn't ask how Dannie acquired such a house. Was it legitimate and legal? I didn't want to know then, and I wasn't sure I wanted to know now.

The van moved away from us and was pulled into the compound of a gated estate, stopping in front of an imposing wooden entrance framed by sleek black and honey-colored granite walls.

"Come inside," Dannie said, his voice smooth as he led the way, past the grand doors into the house. The interior hadn't changed much—it was exactly how I remembered it.

The mansion felt like a scaled-down, contemporary take on Buckingham Palace. Every room here was curated with a different style, each one more lavish than the last. From the Ming dynasty antiques to sleek modern furnishing, the decor was stunning clash of styles that somehow worked together.

"Wow," Wendy murmured, her eyes wide as she took

in the opulence. "I've seen a lot of mansions, but this one... I can't put my finger on it."

That was exactly how I felt the first time I came here. I'd grown up in large houses, but this place was something else. It had the same commanding presence as the British Museum—like it didn't just represent wealth, but also history and privilege.

"This house was once owned by a lord." Dannie said casually, as if that explained everything.

"Like a British lord? From *Bridgerton*?" Wendy's voice held a teasing lilt.

I couldn't remember if Dannie had told me that detail before. Maybe I'd been too overwhelmed, too busy trying to absorb, to soak in every inch of the place, knowing even then that it wasn't the kind of thing I'd forget.

"Yes," he confirmed.

"Man, that's so hot," Wendy sighed, leaning toward me with a grin.

I raised an eyebrow. "What? you find British men hot now?"

"Well, for a British *lord*?" She fanned herself theatrically.

The open floor plan of the house made it easy to see almost everything from the entrance. To the right was an expansive living area with a plush leather sofas and a grand piano gleaming beneath an enormous crystal chandelier. On the left, a sweeping staircase curved elegantly toward the second floor. Further back, the dining room stretched out, with a sleek, modern kitchen tucked discreetly beside it. Two doors lined the far wall—

one leading to the main kitchen, the other to the back garden.

Floor-to-ceiling windows framed the entire left side of the house, overseeing the swimming pool and a pool house that looked more luxurious than most people's actual home.

We ended up in the dining area, which was furnished with understated elegance. The Ming dynasty-style pieces contrasted sharply with the sleekness of the rest of the house, but they fit the room perfectly. At the center stood a massive, round table with a lazy Susan large enough to hold a feast.

Dannie lowered himself into a chair facing the front door, a position of authority, then he gestured for me to take the seat next to him.

"Not here." Dannie's sharp, sudden tone made Wendy jump as her hand brushed the back of the chair next to his. "Over there, next to June."

Dannie's grandma descended from the staircase, poised and elegant in a champagne-colored day dress. Beside her walked a young woman in her late teens, her dark locks cut into a sleek bob. As soon as they reached the bottom step, Dannie moved quickly to his grandmother's side, taking her other arm—the one not already held by the young woman.

Wendy had just settled herself comfortably next to me. I stood up but remained beside my chair. The old lady only had two arms, and a third person wasn't going to make her walk any faster or steadier, so I stayed where I was.

"Oh, oh..." Dannie's grandmother broke into a warm

smile as she reached me, wrapping me in a surprisingly firm embrace.

"So happy. So happy," she repeated, her voice soft but bright with emotion.

"Hey, you don't remember me?" The young woman stepped forward, pulling me into a hug I couldn't refuse. I searched my memory, but nothing came up. "It's me. Laura."

"Laura? The little girl?"

Ten years ago, she had been just a little girl. That was why I couldn't place her. She was the girl who used to follow Dannie's grandmother around. The girl his grandmother had insisted his mother adopt after Dannie's sister died in the incident with his father, hoping Laura could be a replacement daughter. Sadly, it hadn't worked. His mother couldn't bear the grief and took her own life soon after.

"Lola, *cha, cha.*" Grandma instructed, her voice gentle but firm. With swift, practiced movements, Laura performed an intricate tea ritual, gracefully pouring the steaming liquid into tiny, delicate cups before serving each of us.

"Laura learned how to make tea from a Sifu in Hang Zhou," Dannie explained, downing his cup in one smooth motion. "Now Grandma has to have it every day."

"Hmm, not bad," he mused, setting the cup back down. "But the fragrance is lacking. What tea is it?"

"Oolong," Laura answered, her tone respectful.

"Where's the Pu-er I bought?"

"Mama wouldn't drink it."

A rapid exchange followed in Cantonese between

Dannie and his grandmother, their words fluid and intense. Eventually, Laura slipped away to fetch the tea Dannie preferred while the rest of us sat in awkward silence.

Dannie resumed translating as his grandmother's attention shifted to Wendy. She seemed unusually curious about her, her questions thoughtful but persistent. Then, to our surprise, she addressed Wendy in a few words of Hindi.

Wendy's face lit up in recognition. She replied in kind before switching back to English.

"My parents didn't teach me much Hindi," she admitted, her voice tinged with regret. "But I'm curious—how did you learn?"

Dannie stepped in to explain. "Grandma used to work for a British company with extensive trade ties to India."

"Wait—does that mean you speak English?" I asked, realizing too late that my tone sounded more like an interrogation. I softened my voice. "Sorry, I mean... you must've picked up some English, right?"

"Of course." Her smile deepened as she answered, her English accent crisp and refined—reminiscent of the voices in old black-and-white British films. "I just like to hear my grandson speaking in English."

"Oh my, your accent is so wonderful. Nobody speaks like this anymore." My admiration was genuine, and she acknowledged it with a graceful nod.

Both Laura and Dannie spoke fluent English, but their accents were a curious blend of British precision and American casualness. It would be hard to place their nationality by voice alone, but it was clear they had attended an English-speaking school.

Out of nowhere, Grandma Wu gave a deliberate, unmistakable cough—the kind designed to draw attention. The room fell silent. Five long, charged seconds passed.

Then she spoke, her words cutting through the air. "When are you two going to have a baby?"

10

June

Kai's grandma stared straight into my soul. Her gaze was stern, intense, and unwavering. There was no doubt the question was directed at me, as if having children was solely my responsibility. In my experience, I had met single women who wanted children without any partners interfering, but even they needed help from medical professionals.

A sudden shout from far away rescued me from the awkwardness. If she stared at me any longer, I was sure my soul would be sucked out of my body. Still, her message was clear: she expected me to stick around and provide her with grandchildren.

The two thugs who had been waiting outside the grocery store stormed in. One of them tripped over the centerpiece of an antique-looking table, nearly knocking over an equally old yellow-and-green oriental-style vase.

"Mou lai mao, chow dun ba bai," Grandma said in

Cantonese, this time directing her words at Dannie. I couldn't understand why she wouldn't speak English to him now that both Wendy and I knew she was fluent.

The two men shrank under her glare, hurriedly bowing their heads in apology. Dannie gestured for the one called Tiger to come closer. Tiger leaned in and whispered something into his ear.

Grandma replied in Cantonese, her voice sharp with irritation.

I couldn't make out what Tiger was saying, but I was impressed that Grandma could. Even if I had heard the words clearly, I wouldn't have understood most of them. They were speaking too fast and exclusively in Cantonese. Maybe it was easier for them to communicate in their native tongue—or maybe they didn't want their foreign guests to understand the conversation.

Either way, it was obvious that whatever had happened was a problem for Dannie, and it had angered his grandma.

"I think we should get going," I said, seizing the opportunity to escape the tense atmosphere. Wendy had been trying to tell me something earlier, and I hoped it was news about Kai. Good or bad, I needed to know.

"No, you stay," Grandma commanded, her voice loud, cutting through the room like a blade.

"Alright," I muttered, sinking back into my seat.

She continued speaking in rapid Cantonese. Dannie simply sat there, letting her take the lead. I wondered if all Asian grandmothers wielded this kind of power over their families. My mother certainly did. Whenever she was around, she dominated the room, dictating how people should behave, think and even breathe. Once, she told my dad's new wife to shut her mouth and stop breathing through it.

Laura intervened, offering to show us around the house. I jumped at the chance. Wendy, however, hesitated, clearly curious to see how the confrontation would unfold. I had to step on her toes to get her moving.

"What was going on?" I asked as we climbed the stairs, finally out of sight.

"Oh, you don't understand Cantonese?" Laura tilted her head.

"No." I admitted.

"Neither do I," Wendy chimed in, suddenly pushing her face uncomfortably close to Laura. "What were they saying?"

"Wendy," I hissed, shooting her a warning glare. She could hear Laura just fine without invading her personal space.

Laura chuckled softly. "When you said you wanted to leave, I thought you understood at least some of it."

"No. My mother knows a bit of Cantonese, but she never bothered to teach me."

Laura pushed open a set of ornate double doors. "This is where Lord Whiteshire used to host his tea parties. Well, technically, his wife did."

The room was grand and stately, bathed in the soft glow of sunlight streaming through large windows framed by heavy, floor-to-ceiling navy blue curtains. The walls were adorned with a wallpaper veined with gold, in a slightly darker shade of navy blue. In the center of the ceiling hung an opulent chandelier, its crystals sparkling like captured stars. Three elegant couches formed a seating area: a three-seater in the middle and two smaller ones on either side.

"Are the furnishings from the Victorian era?" I asked, more to keep Laura talking than out of genuine curiosity. In my experience, people tended to reveal more when they were in the mood to chat.

"God, no," she laughed. "These are new. The old ones were ancient, and Grandma was convinced someone died on one of them."

"Really?" I forced out a chuckle, hoping to keep her talking.

"Yeah. I was too young to remember moving into this house, but that stuck with me. For me, it was kind of hilarious, you know?"

"How so?"

She grinned. "I always thought old people weren't supposed to be scared of ghosts."

"Oh, I thought it was the opposite. What I heard was that young children aren't afraid of ghosts."

"Yeah, that's because they don't know what ghosts are," she swallowed hard, "until they realize what they are."

"You sound like you have experience with this. Care to share?"

"Gosh, why are you guys always talking about ghosts? First haunted buildings, now haunted furniture. Can we please steer away from that topic? I'm not a big fan of this weird culture of yours." Wendy circled her index finger at us, her head followed the direction of the twirl.

A soft knock on the double wooden doors made all

our heads turn. Laura nodded to a middle-aged woman in a white polo shirt and black pants holding a tray of tea. She was accompanied by four other people—two men and two women—dressed similarly, though their polo shirts were light gray.

"Thank you, Ling Jie.".

Ling Jie smiled kindly at the acknowledgment, and her team quickly got to work. Within a minute, the coffee tables were filled with beautiful miniature cakes, biscuits, scones, and delicate finger sandwiches.

"Grandma must have decided to move the tea party up here," Laura mused.

We heard raised voices coming from downstairs. The tension in the air thickened.

"What's really going on?" I pressed, leaning in closer. "You can tell me. Dannie and I don't have secrets."

I knew that wasn't entirely true. But Dannie had never lied to me, at least, not directly.

"Okay. So, when Dad died," she blinked twice, "I mean, when Dannie's dad died, he took over."

"Yes, I knew that." I reached for her hands, squeezing them gently. "I'm sure he would be proud to have you as his daughter."

"Thanks. It's just that..." She looked up at me, her eyes glistening with unshed tears, "Dannie... well, only Grandma ever acknowledges my existence in this family."

"Dannie is just an emotionally unavailable asshole, isn't he?"

Laura giggled softly. "You're funny. I like you a lot."

"Thank you. Now, you were saying..." My curiosity gnawed at me, and I needed to find out more.

"Yeah, you were saying..." Wendy chimed in, just as eager.

"Dannie's uncle was busted for drug dealing and spent years in prisons. Now he's finally out, and he wants Dannie to hand over the family businesses to him."

"I see. What does your grandma think about it?"

"Grandma doesn't believe a drug addict should be allowed anywhere near the family business."

"He's an addict?"

"He was—until he went to prison. But as soon as he got out, he was back on it again."

"Is he dangerous?"

"He is loud. And he makes a lot of threats, you know? But people always do that with Dannie—and our family. I'm kind of used to it."

I couldn't help feeling sad for her. Growing up in America, my biggest fear had been school shootings—rare as they were back in my day. My parents had always thought I was being silly.

But for Laura, the threat wasn't hypothetical or random. It was real. People targeted her family simply because of who they were.

"Will he hurt Dannie?"

I couldn't wrap my head around the fact that Dannie had to protect himself from his own flesh and blood.

"No," Laura shook her head, "maybe he'd try, but no one can get near Dannie without being tackled down first."

"What about you and Dannie's grandmother?"

She let out a heavy sigh. "I like to think he wouldn't

hurt his own mother. But who knows? People do all sorts of crazy things when they're high."

"Has he ever tried to hurt you?"

"Only once." She pulled her hands from mine, her voice quieting. "I don't think he'll try again. Grandma promised she won't let it happen to me as long as she's alive."

"I'm sorry about what happened. You can tell me everything if you want to."

"Maybe one day."

When a loud crash echoed from downstairs, my patience snapped. I couldn't sit there any longer. The elegant spread of treats wasn't enough to hold my attention. My curiosity—and worry for Dannie—overpowered everything else.

Laura tried to distract me with idle conversation, but I barely heard her. Where I bought my clothes was none of her business, and frankly, I didn't care where she shopped either.

"June, June!" She kept calling my name as I strode down the corridor toward the marble staircase.

All I knew was that if I couldn't stop something bad from happening to Kai, the least I could do was prevent whatever was brewing downstairs. Whatever it was, I had to stop it.

No one seemed to notice my arrival. They were too busy arguing with each other in a language I did not understand. As I carefully snuck past the intimidating, tattooed men, I realized that most of them were carrying weapons—machetes, baseball bats, and what looked like the metal bars police used to control riots.

A sudden wave of anxiety crashed over me. It felt like I was walking a tightrope, fifteen stories above the ground. When I spotted Dannie, he gave me a slight nod, and his eyes never left me as I tiptoed my way to him.

Laura was gone. She had stopped following me when I reached the bottom of the stairs. I was just relieved I wouldn't have to hear her telling me I shouldn't be here. Anyway, Wendy would handle her. She had a way with people—even when her words were sharp and offensive, no one ever seemed to stay mad at her for long.

Finally, I reached Dannie's side, feeling like I had completed an obstacle course. The only difference was that I wasn't covered in mud—and this was far more dangerous.

The argument halted abruptly as a man in his fifties jabbed a finger toward me and shouted something. I had no evidence he was directing his anger at me, but the language barrier did nothing to ease my nerves.

"She only speaks English," Dannie explained.

"Hello, bitch. You the wife?" the man sneered.

"Yes, and you are..." The words escaped before I could stop them, and I immediately regretted admitting I was Dannie's wife in front of all these thugs. If they hadn't known who I was before, they did now.

"Dannie's uncle. Kneel and serve me tea." He chuckled darkly. "You owe me."

"She doesn't owe you anything." Gone was the kind, grandmotherly demeanor as Dannie's grandmother stepped forward, exuding a fierce authority. "No one owes you anything. But... We'll give you something, a business. Work on it. Sell it. I don't care. Your father wouldn't care."

She tilted her head slightly, and Dannie leaned to listen. After a brief pause, he spoke, his voice devoid of emotion. "You can have the nightclub on Jordan Road."

"That—"

"That's more than enough for now," she cut him off. "After a year, if things go well, we can negotiate again."

"Fine," he spat, turning on his heel and leaving. Eight or ten others left with him. I couldn't understand how someone fresh out of jail still held so much power and loyalty.

Only then did I realize that an even larger group remained. I hadn't had the chance to do a proper head-count, but there had to be at least fifty people left. My gaze fell on shattered pieces of colorful ceramic shattered across the floor. A maid emerged swiftly with a broom and dustpan, cleaning the mess with practiced efficiency.

"I apologize on behalf of my son," Dannie's grand-mother said, bowing slightly.

"Please, it's okay." I replied, unsure of what else to say. Despite her kindness, she radiated an aura of authority that made me feel compelled to reassure her that every-thing was okay.

"Since the cat is out of the bag, maybe you should show her around," she suggested.

"I will," Dannie answered.

I wondered what she wanted Dannie to show me. It didn't seem like she meant the house, because five minutes later, Dannie's van was waiting for us outside. She excused herself, claiming the need for an afternoon nap, and bid me goodbye.

The drive was quiet. I didn't say a word to Dannie. I

wished Wendy had come with us. She would have said something, cracked a joke to break the tense silence. But she had stayed behind with Laura. None of us had a choice. It seemed Dannie's grandmother really wanted us to spend some alone time together.

"This is us," Dannie said as the van stopped in front of a tall, sleek, modern office building. The doorman immediately slid open the van door and greeted him.

"Mrs. Wu," Dannie smirked as he got out of the van.

"You're having too much fun with this, aren't you?" I asked, arching an eyebrow.

"Yes, I am."

I shook my head as the doorman bowed, treating me like royalty. Another doorman held open the building's entrance.

"Where are we?" I asked as we stepped inside.

"My office. All my businesses are here." If he hadn't told me, I would have assumed we had entered a cooperate headquarters or high-end financial firm on Wall Street.

One of the eight elevators arrived, held open by the first doorman. Dannie and I stepped inside, while the others remained outside. He pressed the button for the second floor, and moments later, we were greeted by a gleaming display of a well-known Asian skincare brand, their promotional posters lining the walls.

"Is this your floor?"

"Yes, and the rest of it."

"What do you mean?"

"The whole building, duh?" *Duh?* Was it that obvious?

I shook my head. "Why do you need the entire building?"

"Investment, of course. In Hong Kong, the best investment is land and property."

"What about all these businesses? Are they just a front for your operation?" I air-quoted the word 'businesses' and 'operation'.

He smirked.

"Why do you talk like that?" He mimicked my air quotes, exaggerating every word.

I couldn't help but roll my eyes at him.

"On second floor is a branding and marketing company," he continued. "We have a team of just under a hundred—everything from design to strategy experts."

"So, you don't own that beauty brand?" I gestured the elevator. "You know, the poster out there."

"No, we designed the posters—along with everything else you see in Asia."

Leena Beauty was one of the newest and biggest beauty brands in Asia, known for its bold marketing campaigns. I hadn't even heard of them until I started travelling to Asia for business. Their posters were everywhere—covering every inch of available advertising space.

"Legit business, huh?"

"Do you approve?" Dannie couldn't hide his smile as he added, "Wife."

I just flatted my lips and glared at him.

He led me through more floors, each one occupied by one of his businesses. On the eighth floor was a Japanese street food and franchise. He had acquired the master rights and now ran over 500 stores across Hong Kong, Singapore, Vietnam, and Malaysia.

Another floor held one of his proudest ventures, a karaoke chain. It had started with a single humble location and expanded into a massive success, with outlets in every major mall across Asia. He beamed as he showed me a bright red booth that resembled a classic London telephone box. Inside, a karaoke machine connected to a microphone and headphones stood in the soundproofed space.

"You can choose to sing for as little as ten minutes," he explained, demonstrating how to work the screen. "Then, you just sing your heart out. No worries, no judgment."

He showed me a few other floors, each more impressive than the last: a financial firm that handled investments, a fashion design studio specializing in modernized Chinese costumes, a property management company offering all-in-one services for Airbnb owners, a funeral home, and even a car dealership. These were just a handful of the businesses he chose to show me.

He leased the remaining floors out to friends he trusted.

Our tour ended on the 28th floor—his office. This was the headquarters of his management company, the center of everything he owned.

"Can you see now?" he asked quietly.

I nodded. "It's very impressive."

"I've gone legit."

"I can see that."

His voice softened, a rare vulnerability slipping through. "Would you still leave me?"

11

Kai

Five long hours later, we finally arrived at Hong Kong International airport. If we had taken my private jet, we would have made it in three. Sometimes, I enjoyed a good commercial flight—feeling what a normal person experiences when they travel humbled me greatly.

I had no idea what had happened to Jenny at the house. Did we kill her husband? Everything happened so quickly that it was a blur. All I could recall was his helpless face and lifeless body lying there in a pool of his own blood.

Trevon, Clare, and I stood in the exceptionally long queue at the taxi rank. My patience wore thin when one of the children in front of us fell on me during their tug-of-war. Clare, ever loyal, would have gladly done some serious damage if I had asked her to.

Did I hate children?

I tried my best to be nice to Jenny's kids. I did. But they simply didn't warm my heart the way dogs did.

"Couldn't you just order a car from your phone?" I finally asked Trevon, the question burning me inside.

"Why didn't you do it?" Trevon challenged.

"Do you want me to, Sir?" Clare volunteered, still remarkably polite. She would remain that way as long as I remained pissed at her.

"Well, I would, but you know I don't have my phone on me." I said to Trevon.

"Would you? Do you even know how to do it?" He teased, his lips pursed as he tried to hide his amusement.

I shot him a glare. "Of course."

I believed I could if I had to, but truthfully, I had never done it myself.

"I think it's best we keep our steps untraceable."

I nodded, choosing to agree to disagree. I couldn't be bothered to argue with him right now. If the police were looking for me, it wouldn't take them long. They knew I had flown to Hong Kong on a commercial flight. CCTV would reveal how I left the airport and trace me from there.

When we finally got into a taxi, Trevon told the driver to take us to a hotel I had never stayed in before, one I had deliberately avoided. Thirty minutes later, we arrived in Tsim Sha Tsui. While we checked in, Clare offered to conduct a search. Trevon, ever cautious, used a pseudonym to check us into the hotel.

Bobbie Brown.

"Bobbie? Really?" I raised an eyebrow.

"Shut the fuck up," he shot back.

I held down the burning questions swirling in my mind as Trevon paid in cash. The nice young lady at the check-in desk couldn't seem to stop eyeing us. I wondered what was going through her head. Did she think we were a couple? Or had she figured out that Trevon didn't exactly look like a Bobbie?

Fifteen minutes later, we reached our room.

Yes. Room. Singular.

"Spit it all out now," Trevon demanded, arms crossed over his chest. "I know you're dying inside."

I flopped onto the large double bed, leaning back slightly as I kicked off my shoes. "One room? Really? I didn't realize you missed our roommate days so much."

"I only have one fake ID with me."

I chuckled despite myself. "Bobbie Brown? Seriously? You could have at least gotten a twin room."

"I didn't have a choice. The fake passport was ready-made, and they just stuck my photo on it." He unfastened his tie.

"Yes, haven't you heard? I'm in love with you," he added with a wink, lightening the tension from today's disaster.

"I thought you didn't touch anything illegal. How did you manage to get a fake ID?"

"Oh boy, you don't know everything about me."

"Apparently not." I folded my arms across my chest. He had changed, and I wasn't pleased with myself for not noticing.

"This isn't the right time to dive into my life story."

As much as I agreed with him, I wanted to catch up with my best friend, the one I had clearly lost touch with over the past few years. "Well, if we're sharing a room tonight, we've got all night."

"Fine, we do have some time. I help smuggle people out of trouble now and then. You happy?"

"Fuck, are you trafficking people?" My stomach twisted with images of innocent women tied up and sold to horrible places.

"No. Fuck no. I help refugees get to safety, provide a place to stay—things like that."

Relief washed over me, and I scolded myself for jumping to conclusions.

"Wow, that's surprisingly noble of you." I wanted to know more but pushed that curiosity aside. "Why did you pick this hotel? Isn't this place run by a triad?"

I might not know everything about Hong Kong, but as a businessman, I knew which places to avoid. The Hong Kong Triads topped that list. They were brutal, reckless, and the kind of people I didn't want to cross.

"That is why I used a fake name," Trevon replied, avoiding my actual question.

I sighed. "Tell me exactly why you picked this place."

"Fine, don't panic." He tiled his head, the hint of a smirk playing on his lips, "June and Wendy are here."

"What?" Suddenly, everything made sense. Trevon wouldn't have brought me here unless it involved June. Or Wendy.

"Yes, you heard me. They're here."

"Why didn't you tell me you were in contact with them?" Had we really drifted apart so much? He no longer wanted to share with me everything he knew.

"Only Wendy."

"Still. It's better than nothing. I haven't heard from June since…"

How long had it been? Two days? My memory was a mess.

"Can you call her? I want to talk to June."

"No, she's not in a place to talk right now."

"What do you mean?"

"She usually replies quickly, but not today. Something's up. I can feel it."

"Tell me what you already know."

"They tried all day to get a fake visa but couldn't. So, they went to see June's ex."

I stood up, tension prickling at the back of my neck. "What? How the hell is her ex supposed to help?"

"She didn't say. There were only three messages since they left for Hong Kong."

"Which are…?"

"Fuck, you are controlling."

"Spit it out." I wolfed down half a mini bottle of Tsingtao beer.

"Look," he handed me his phone, and I took it. "Don't scroll any further than today," he warned.

First message: Hun, Trent told me everything. I'm on my way to find Kai in Shanghai.

Second message: Tried many places. No one would help us. Think we're going to try June's ex.

Third message: Found Kai. How's everything going over there?

Fourth message: Meet me here. Below this message is the pin of our current location.

"Four messages," I blurted out.

"What?"

"You said three."

"Okay, four. I miscounted. I'm sorry, my lord."

I wanted to know when Wendy and June would join us—if they were going to get in touch anytime soon. But there was no point grilling Trevon for information that he clearly didn't have. I had seen his phone.

We took the time to call Trent and updated him on our situation. He then briefly told me what happened over there, including how Dave was attacked at the airport. Trent already had some people searching for Dave, but I decided to have Clare set up another search team as well. I couldn't bear the idea of losing my favorite bodyguard.

However, it was strange—why would someone target Dave and my innocent June?

Approximately two hours later, Trevon received a text from Wendy. She and June were both at a party in the grand ballroom, and she would find an opportunity to sneak out and meet us.

I couldn't wait any longer. We had been sitting ducks, anxiously waiting to hear from them. Every time Trevon's phone made a noise, my heart leaped, only to be disappointed when it wasn't Wendy.

I couldn't help but wonder if June had tried to contact me. Without my phone, there was no way to know. Trevon had tried calling it, but it went straight to voice mail.

"I'm going to find her," I declared, ignoring Trevon's advice to get some rest. My body and mind simply wouldn't allow it.

I jumped up and began searching for the shoes I had kicked off earlier.

"I don't think that's a good idea. We don't even know where they are," Trevon argued.

"We could split into two teams. We'd find them faster that way," I suggested.

"Right. And how am I supposed to contact you if I find them first? Huh?"

"What makes you think you'll find them first?"

"Well, the chances are fifty-fifty."

He had a point. My fondness for June made me think I would be the one to find her. Maybe it was desperation. I wanted so badly to see her again.

Things had spiraled out of control over the past few days. My cousin was in serious trouble, her husband was dead—possibly murdered by her, or even by me. Depends on which angle you looked at the situation from. Jail was a looming possibility.

I couldn't let anything happen to June too.

"How about we go together?" Trevon suggested. "Clare can search on her own and call us if she finds them first."

We agreed to his plan. Clare would check the hotel's five bars and restaurants, while Trevon and I headed to the ballroom.

When we reached the first floor, we discovered there was only one party happening that night, located in the grand ballroom. There was no sign outside of the door. Typically, the hotel displayed signs for birthdays, weddings, or other celebrations, but tonight, nothing.

The only indication of a party were the two guards

posted outside, scanning every visitor who entered and exited.

Trevon and I decided to pull an old trick that had worked for us many times back in college: the drunken monkeys. We wrinkled our suits, messed up our hair, linked arms and stumbled into things, walking crookedly to the entrance. I half-laughed and half-shouted while Trevon giggled, slurring words that made no sense.

The taller guard with military haircut barked something in Cantonese. The younger guard, whose hair was perfectly gelled, spoke in English. "This is a private party."

"I'm a guess, damn it," Trevon slurred.

Though my Cantonese was limited, I caught bits of their conversation. Military Hair was flexing his chest muscles, complaining that he was bored and wanted to beat us up. Hair Gel disagreed, arguing that unless they called for backup, they couldn't both leave their post. They mentioned something about their boss.

A smartly dressed couple arrived. The short, bald man nodded at the guards and mentioned his name. Immediately, the guards transformed, offering warm smiles and a welcoming demeanor that we didn't witness earlier. Hair Gel opened the door wide for the couple, while Military Hair stood firmly in our way. Preventing us from sneaking past the door.

Taking advantage of the situation, Trevon and I tried to sneak a peek inside. We continued our drunken act, bouncing on our toes and flailing our arms as if we were trying to climb over the guards.

"Let's find another party. This one isn't fun," Trevon said, tugging me away from the door.

"But I want to go to this one," I pouted, digging in my heels.

"I'm Mr. Chen Gong." I shouted in Mandarin.

I had no proof that Jenny's husband had been invited to this party, but he was a notorious party boy. If anyone could get into an exclusive event, it would have been him. Name-dropping was worth a shot—even if, at this very moment, he might not be breathing.

"Mr. Chen?"

"Yes." I was starting to think my trick had worked.

"This is your…?" Military Hair asked in his not-very-fluent Mandarin.

"New toy," Trevon added, as he planted a kiss on my forehead.

"Ah ha, you like it strong and black," Hair Gel quipped, his tone laced with casual racism. Military Hair laughed. I wanted to tell them to mind their manners, but this wasn't the time to lecture uncultured people about respect and diversity.

"Wait, I don't think you're on the list," Hair Gel said, his suspicious gaze scanning us.

"Impossible," I snapped.

"This is a very private event," he continued, "I don't think—"

For a moment, I questioned if these guards actually had some brainpower. They weren't just here to intimidate people.

"Look, I just happened to be in Hong Kong and heard about this party—"

"Honey, I'm sad," Trevon interrupted, raising his voice to an exaggerated, high-pitched whine that sent an involuntary shiver down my spine. I silently prayed he wouldn't do it again.

"Look what you've done. Now my baby is sad. I'm leaving tomorrow. If he's not happy, then I'm not happy—and if I'm unhappy, your boss won't be happy," Trevon added, his words an illogical mess. But two drunken idiots weren't supposed to make sense.

"Yeah, the boss is going to be pissed if you make a scene," Military Hair mumbled to Hair Gel before switching to a mix of English and Mandarin. "His wife is back from America, and he won't let anyone ruin this party. Not even someone like you."

"June." Her name escaped my lips before I realized it.

"You heard?" Hair Gel's eyes narrowed with interest.

"Let me in," I demanded, attempting to push past them. Trevon, surprisingly, was the one who held me back this time. Both guards stared at us like we were some kind of absurd puppet show.

"Let's go," Trevon said firmly.

I couldn't fight him. One, he was remarkably strong. Two, I hadn't properly slept in days and was too exhausted to resist. When he finally loosened his deadly grip on my arm, we were in a quiet corridor, away from the guards.

"Listen to me, buddy," Trevon said, slapping my face. Hard.

"What the hell was that for?" I rubbed my stinging cheek, the burn spreading like a trail of ants.

"You're not listening!"

"Fine," I growled.

"Did you see those guards?"

"Yes. Didn't you? What's your point?"

"They aren't just any guards. Can't you tell?"

Now that he mentioned it, things started to click. Military Hair had a jagged scar across his scalp, and Hair Gel sported a neck tattoo that no tailored suit could fully conceal. Plenty of people had scars and tattoos, but here, in this hotel, it meant something else. I had been so eager to get inside that I missed the danger standing right in front of me.

"What are you implying?" I asked, though I already had a sinking suspicion.

I thought I knew what Trevon was saying, but I needed to hear it from him. This was the last place I ever wanted to be. I'd avoided anything to do with criminals since the day I was kidnapped. Every time I worked with these people, I wrestled with my inner demons. Some of them could be nice, sure—but I couldn't shake the feeling that one day they'd turn on me. Betray me. Stab me in the back when I wasn't looking.

"I think you know," Trevon said.

"The host. The boss," I murmured, realization dawning. "Someone powerful in the triad."

"Exactly my thoughts," he confirmed.

If the guards were telling the truth, then June was in serious trouble. "The American girl. The wife... It's June."

"Or coincidence?" Trevon offered weakly.

I refused to believe in coincidence. Not here. Not now.

"Are you kidding me?" I raised my hand, ready to slap him back for his earlier assault.

"Sorry, sorry," he said quickly, raising his hands in surrender. "I was trying to be optimistic, but you're right. I think that's your June."

"We need to get her out."

"And Wendy," Trevon reminded me.

"Yes," I agreed, feeling guilty because I kept forgetting that Wendy had been swept into this whole mess because of June, and I couldn't leave her behind.

"We need to get back to our room," he said urgently.

"Why?"

He held up his phone. A text from Wendy blinked on the screen. **See you in five.**

12

———

June

The door opened before either Wendy or I had the chance to knock. Without hesitation, Kai leaned in to hug me. It was a long hug—much longer than five Mississippis. More like fifteen Mississippis.

Trevon coughed, breaking the moment.

"We should probably move inside," he suggested, glancing down the hallway.

Standing at the door hugging would definitely attract attention. I had no idea when Dannie would notice that Wendy and I had been gone far too long for a simple bathroom trip.

I fought the overwhelming urge to kiss Kai, but with Trevon and Wendy watching, a sudden shyness crept over me. It wasn't as if they didn't know how I felt about Kai—it was obvious—but expressing affection in front of others was hard for me. Even with an audience of just two.

Room 1202 was a standard hotel room overlooking the busy streets of Hong Kong. The faint hum of traffic filtered through the window. It was so ordinary that I couldn't help but wonder what had been on Kai's mind when he booked it. He was used to the best life had to offer—luxury suites, private villas. This room felt beneath him. Had he really chosen to book this room himself?

"I'm so sorry." His voice was soft but urgent. I couldn't believe those were the first words out of his mouth. "I shouldn't have left without saying goodbye. I panicked. I had a nervous breakdown. I was afraid something might have happened to Jenny. I couldn't think—I couldn't function the moment you left me after lunch."

He started to ramble, his words spilling out faster, a whirlwind of guilt and anxiety. I reached up and pressed a finger gently against his lips, shushing him softly.

"It's okay," I whispered, repeating it a few more times until he finally fell silent. I guided him to the edge of the bed and sat us both down.

Deep down, I had always known he had to leave. But when I realized he'd disappeared, my own demons had taken control—my fear of abandonment, the ache left behind when Chloe disappeared without a trace. The thought of losing Kai the same way had made me mad. Had I always been this fragile? This scared?

"I'm so glad to see you," I murmured. My lips betrayed me, brushing against the corner of his mouth in a soft, impulsive kiss.

"Me too," he said, his voice thick with emotion. "So much has happened. I wish you had been with me through it all."

"I would go anywhere with you." The words slipped out of my mouth before I could stop them. Would I really, though? Could I leave everything behind—my patients, my responsibilities—if he asked me to? Would I abandon an open operating table if he needed me?

Kai shook his head, a faint smile tugging at his lips.

"No, no. As much as I want you by my side, I still have some sense." He reached up, brushing a stray lock of hair —one rebellious strand escaping from the elegant updo Laura's stylist had perfected—off my face. "It wouldn't be fair to drag you into my mess."

"Tell me what happened," I urged softly.

He hesitated.

"It's a long story," he said finally. "Why don't you tell me how you ended up here?"

He hadn't mentioned Dannie's name, but I could tell that's what he meant. He knew.

Out of the corner of my eye, I caught a glimpse of Wendy and Trevon near the entrance. The room wasn't large, and they were doing their best to give us some privacy while staying within earshot.

"Nothing important," I said. "I came looking for you."

Kai's expression softened. "Trev told me you couldn't get to Shanghai."

"It was foolish of me to think I could just march into your hometown and find you."

"Maybe. But thank you for coming anyway." His grin lit up his face, a rare brightness cutting through the dark circles beneath his eyes. "It means a lot to know you care."

Our gaze locked, and the air between us thickened. My heart pounded as our faces drifted closer together— so close it would've been ridiculous not to close the distance.

And then we did.

The kiss was hot. Hungry. Desperate.

The world outside the room faded. My body melted into his touch as his lips claimed mine. I felt whole again—complete. And yet, somehow, it still wasn't enough.

I wanted more. Needed more.

My tongue teased against his, tasting him, savoring him like a forbidden delicacy.

He responded instantly, matching my hunger with his own. When I pressed closer, he leaned back, pulling me with him. Before I could catch my breath, his arm curled around my waist, and in one swift motion, he flipped me onto the bed.

A soft gasp escaped my lips as my back hit the mattress. The heat between us burned hotter, and as his body hovered over mine, all I could think about was how much I wanted to lose myself in him.

Our lips were no longer touching. Kai's breath came faster, and his eyes bored into mine, hunger setting his gaze on fire. But he closed his eyes, and I felt the room rush back in. "Slow down tiger."

I pouted in protest.

"We're going for a walk," came Wendy's voice, followed by the sound of the door shutting. I giggled, the memory of the moment we shared in the ballroom came back to me still fresh and vivid.

This here? This wasn't me.

Whenever I was with Kai, I wasn't June. At least, not the June I recognized.

Wild. Ruthless. Passionate. Those weren't words anyone would ever use to describe me—not even myself. What else? Sexy? Crazy? Open-minded to life, to any possibility? Not me. Not until him.

"Now, does this count as one of our dates?" I teased, my voice light, playful.

Kai let out a laugh, warm and smooth. "You're funny."

Funny. Another thing no one had ever called me before. I barely recognized myself around him. And I wasn't sure if that scared me or thrilled me.

"Shut up and kiss me," I demanded, pulling his face toward mine. He collapsed next to me on the plush bed, and just like that, we leaned against each other, side by side. Kissing. Pausing only to catch our breath.

One of his hands found its way to my knee, his palm warm against my cool skin. It wasn't cold in Hong Kong, but the air conditioning must have been on full blast. So cold that my nipples stood at attention beneath the silk of my dress—unless they simply wanted attention from a certain someone in the room.

"Nice dress." Kai took the opportunity to comment between breaths. "Apple green looks good on you."

I tilted my head, studying him through half-lidded eyes.

"It's not exactly apple green," I corrected. "More like pastel green. Baby-blanket green."

"Still," he murmured, a teasing smile playing on his lips.

"You look nice too." I winced internally at my clumsy reply. Accepting compliments wasn't my strong suit. Chloe always told me to just say thanks and welcome positivity with open arms. Apparently, returning a compliment diminished the energy people sent out—the energy the universe sent out.

"And I love how smooth this fabric is," he added, letting his fingers trail upward along my thigh.

His touch, slow and deliberate, burned through the delicate material, spreading heat between my legs.

I leaned back, breath hitching as his hand roamed higher. Butterflies fluttered low in my belly, a restless swarm beneath his touch.

"Kiss me again," I whispered, my voice trembling with want. I wanted to melt in his mouth the way he melted me somewhere else.

"Yes, your highness."

I gasped as his teeth found a nipple, shamelessly straining against the fabric of my dress. He cupped my breast, kneading it gently while his mouth worked me into a fever. I didn't think it was possible for my nipples to be any harder—but for him, they were.

My toes curled when he leaned in again, sucking and tugging at the sensitive peak. Electric pressure jolted through my whole body, hot and sudden. I knew he was a playboy, a womanizer, but when this all started, I'd never imagined his touch would feel this good. How could simple touch carry so much magic?

"No underwear again?" he asked, his voice low, rough.

I made a soft noise in response. I had my reasons. Would he understand a woman's battle with visible panty lines? Or that my push-up bra made my boobs pop too much, and I didn't want to seem too busty in this dress? Going without undergarments seemed like the easier choice—as long as I was careful not to accidentally flash anyone.

Without a word, I undid the top button of my Qi Pao. It came undone faster than it had taken to put on. The dress was a work of art, crafted by one of the most renowned Qi Pao tailors in Hong Kong. A good dress should highlight a woman's best feature—tight in all the right places, while enhancing the curves. And this one, with its high side slit, allowed freedom of movement.

His fingers found the core of my heat, sliding against the slick evidence of my desire.

Now, I was beginning to think the split had other purposes too.

I was dying to find out what he would do next. This felt different than the last time we slept together. At that point, I was lusting after Kai, desperate to satisfy the curiosity that had lingered since I was eighteen.

But now—his touch felt different. His body, his warmth, his kiss. Everything about him had changed. It had only been a few days since I last saw him. What changed?

Were we about to make love? The thought seemed ridiculous. No one made love anymore—who had the time and energy? Plenty of my patients came to my clinic not because they couldn't have children, but because they simply didn't have the time to make babies.

A sharp knock at the door shattered the moment.

Kai sighed, pulling away as I sat up and adjusted my dress, smoothing the wrinkles with shaky hands.

He opened the door, and Wendy stood there, her face tense.

"We have to go," she announced. "I think they've started to notice you're missing."

"Who's they?" Kai asked, his voice low and dangerous. "Is that your ex?"

"We should split up," Trevon said, appearing behind Wendy. He tossed something to Kai, who caught it effortlessly. "Clare got this for you. I've already saved the number on my phone—don't lose this one."

Kai examined the burner phone before tucking it into his pocket. "Where are we going?"

"I don't know," Wendy admitted with a shrug. "We'll call Emily and see what she can do."

Kai turned back to me, his hand firm on my shoulder. "What kind of trouble are you in? Answer me."

"I'm not in trouble," I said, and it was the truth. I didn't think Dannie would hurt me. "We just needed to leave. Now."

Wendy's phone buzzed, and she glanced at the screen. "Look, Chloe just texted. She said to head to Mama Bella. It's owned by Matteo."

I stiffened at the name. I knew exactly who Matteo was—the Mafia guy married to Chloe's cousin, Marie. Chloe claimed she hadn't known her family was connected to the Mafia until recently. I wasn't so sure. My trust in her had never fully recovered after her mysterious disappearance.

"Another criminal. Great," I muttered, rolling my eyes. Wendy caught the gesture and raised an eyebrow.

"They're the only people who can help you now," she said, her voice tight.

Kai and I left first. Clare had a car waiting for us at the entrance, nothing flashy, but definitely nicer than an ordinary taxi.

As soon as we were on the road, Kai's voice cut through the silence. "Tell me about your ex."

I swallowed hard, knowing I couldn't avoid this any longer. "Okay, I met him ten years ago during a summer holiday here. We were... kind of married."

His face paled and he swallowed hard while blinking at me rapidly. "Kind of married?"

"We weren't legally married," I clarified quickly. "It was just some ceremony to please his dying grandfather."

Kai let out a harsh breath. "Do you realize that, for some people, that kind of ceremony is an even bigger deal than a legal document?"

I did now. But back then, it hadn't felt real. And right now, that piece of paper—or lack thereof—was the least of my problems.

"Apparently," I admitted. "But we weren't in love, if that helps."

"Are you sure?" His question hung heavy in the air.

"Yes, I'm sure. And I'm not in trouble. Dannie wouldn't hurt me."

"Then why are we running?" His words sliced through my reassurance, and suddenly, the truth hit me harder than I wanted to admit.

This wasn't about me.

"I want to know that too," I said, turning toward him. "What kind of trouble are you in?"

His jaw clenched before he gave me the brief version of the story. By the time we arrived outside Mama Bella, an upscale Italian restaurant, a staff member guided us to a private VIP room tucked discreetly in the back. The dim lighting and polished wooden table suggested this was a place for quiet deals —or secret meetings.

As we waited for Wendy and Trevon, I pressed Kai for more details.

I exhaled slowly. "Jenny must be terrified."

Kai nodded, his expression unreadable.

I was the one that blinked rapidly this time. What was he thinking about that had him so distracted? "You need to help her."

"I don't know what I can do," he confessed.

"We don't know for sure that her husband is dead right?" His gaze sharpened, staring into my skull like I was joking. "It's possible he's still alive."

His hand was warm beneath mine as I reached for him.

"You're not saying that just to comfort me?"

"Yes and no. You'd be surprised what doctors can do these days."

"I feel a lot better." Kai kissed me—slow, deliberate— and without hesitation, I kissed him back.

A knock on the door shattered the fragile intimacy. Trevon and Wendy entered, their faces tense.

I pulled away, heart pounding.

"You should go back," I said softly. "Jenny needs you more than I do."

"I came here for you," Kai countered, his voice rough.

"I don't need saving," I snapped, trying to convince myself as much as him.

Wendy huffed, shaking her head so forcefully it was impossible to ignore.

"You don't get it, do you?" Her tone was razor-sharp. "He's still in love with you."

A chill slid down my spine.

"Dannie?" I asked, though I already knew the answer.

"Yes. Who else?"

I knew Dannie had always liked me—and maybe he was a little protective of me—but love? That was different.

And dangerous.

"You never thought he might still want you?" Trevon cut in, his voice low. "That he is stopping you from leaving?"

"He wouldn't—" I started, but the words fell flat. Wouldn't he?

Kai's jaw clenched. "Why didn't you tell me?"

"Because it doesn't matter," I said, protesting. "He would never hurt me."

"Wouldn't he?" Kai's words sliced through my fragile confidence.

A bitter laugh escaped me. "I already walked away from him once. And he let me go."

"Maybe he regrets it," Wendy murmured. "Men like him? They don't forget. They don't forgive."

The weight of their words settled over me, thick and suffocating.

Kai stepped closer, his voice quieter but no less intense. "What if you're wrong? What if this time, he won't let you go?"

I lifted my chin, defiant. "He has never hurt me and he's not going to start now."

His hand curled around my waist. "How can you be sure?"

"I know what it looks like," I said, wishing they'd just let it all drop.

"Oh wow..." Wendy interrupted.

"Shut the fuck up and let me finish," I snapped at Wendy, and it was about time someone taught her not to interrupt when someone was talking, "Dannie is a very powerful person in Hong Kong. None of us can deny that. His friend is going to help me get a visa tomorrow. His name is Huang An, and he works high up in the department. I just met him at the party."

Everyone in the room looked a little confuse. I knew right away they either didn't believe me, or they didn't believe Dannie would actually help me.

"Look, Dannie and I have history. If I didn't go back to America and become a doctor, I probably would have married him. Just live, never work, have babies for him, and never worry about a thing in the world. But I didn't. I went back to the States, and it was over for us. I know you guys don't trust him, but I do—with my life. He would never hurt me, okay? He would kill for me. He has..."

Wendy gasped while the men didn't seem to react. Kai shot me another look, and I knew he had questions about my past that needed answering.

"It wasn't a big deal." But it was, wasn't it? I've always known that, even if I tried to play it off now.

"What the..." Wendy couldn't help herself. I realized her need to interrupt people couldn't be fixed in one day.

"Someone assaulted me. And before I knew it, you know, Dannie did something..." I kept it brief deliberately. I didn't want to relive that traumatic experience.

"I would do the same for you." Kai wrapped his arms around me, kissing me on the forehead.

I looked up at him. "Do you trust me now? Dannie wouldn't hurt me."

"Okay. I trust your judgement. And if he cares about you that much, then I know at least he can keep you safe. But if he is in love with you, why would he ever let you go? I know I wouldn't."

"Well, he let me go once, right?"

"Yes, he would be an idiot to let you go twice."

"Kai has a point. He could lock you up and have his scary men watch you twenty-four-seven," Wendy chimed in.

"Stop fucking around and wasting your time on me. You guys must realize that Jenny is our priority. Kai needs to go back to Shanghai, go to the police, clear her name, his name—whatever. He won't be able to live with himself if something happens to Jenny."

"I will go with Kai," Trevon volunteered, I smiled at him as he tapped his hand on Kai's shoulder.

"And I'll stay until we meet them in Shanghai." Kai replied, his face dark with worry.

My resolved cracked.

"You have to go," I whispered, though my heart begged him to stay.

"I'll go," he promised. "But this isn't over. Not by a long shot."

13

———

June

"I'm still not sure." Kai blurted out, his head shaking no to what we had already agreed upon.

"What are you not sure about?" Wendy asked, her brow furrowed in concern.

He sighed lightly. "Are you sure you don't have feelings for him?"

I wasn't expecting that from him.

"No, of course not," I said quickly, trying to sound convincing. Too convincing. I realized then that if the answer were true, I wouldn't need to try so hard.

Kai shrugged, then let out a bitter, hysterical laugh. "Can you believe it? Kai Li asking such a stupid question. So fucking pathetic."

"Don't say that."

It had barely been an hour since Kai and I reunited, and already we were questioning and doubting each other. I used to think it was cute when Kai showed his insecure side. In the business world, he was known for his iron will, his ruthlessness, his rigid rules where weakness was unacceptable.

Part of me felt honored to witness the side of him he wouldn't let anyone else see. But another part of me was terrified. What did it all mean? Why did he trust me enough to show me this vulnerable side?

"I've never felt like this for anyone. You make me go crazy." His voice softened as if he were confessing his love for me. Unless I was totally hallucinating.

"I feel the same about you."

Just the sight of him brought a smile to my face. No matter how miserable I was, he could always brighten my world by being there.

"How do you feel about Dannie boy?"

I hesitated for a few seconds. "It's different."

That probably wasn't the answer he wanted to hear.

"Different how?" He let out a dry chuckle that sent chill down my spine. "No, don't answer that."

"Kai." I reached out to touch his shoulder, but he leaned back in his chair, putting distance between us.

"We should leave soon," Kai announced, his tone detached. "Now that these two are no longer in danger, and I'm no longer laying low, am I allowed to use my private jet back to Shanghai? Unless you have something else to tell me?" His voice grew colder, and he was no longer speaking directly to me. Somehow, I had screwed everything up.

I'd started to grow tired of his nonsense. We all knew

he had bigger issues to deal with such as helping Jenny clear her name and to try to get her out of jail. Honestly, I didn't understand why he kept going back and forth about my relationship with Dannie, treating me hot and cold. And I couldn't help but wonder when all of this would end.

Sudden anger surged through me, and I knew this nonsense had to stop—now.

"Dannie made me feel safe." The words slipped out before my brain had time to catch up.

"And I don't?"

"That's not what I mean," I choked out, tears blurring my vision. "He kept me safe when I was away from home, alone. There was a time when nothing I did felt right. My mother didn't approve of the medical school I chose. She wanted me to attend a more prestigious one—someplace where I could leverage the powerful pharmaceutical connections she had meticulously arranged for me. My dad wanted me to do anything else but that—he probably didn't think I had what it took to be a doctor. I felt like a failure. All I needed was some time to myself, so I ran here. To Hong Kong. I thought being around people who looked like me would make me feel safe."

I wiped tears off my cheek. "But I was wrong because I didn't speak a word of Cantonese or Mandarin. People assumed I was a fake, a pretender. Then I met this American guy, but he... he..." My breath hitched as a hiccup threatened to escape. "He wasn't a friend. He violated me in a dark alley. If it weren't for Dannie finding me that night, I would have ended my life then and there."

"Oh, sweetie," Kai murmured as he stood and wrapped me in his arms. "I'm so sorry. I feel like such an idiot."

"In so many ways, he saved me. I couldn't speak for days. I had lost all hopes, and he let me stay at his house while I got better."

"I'm so sorry," he repeated, his hand reaching up to stroke my hair gently.

Anger surged through me suddenly, and I pushed him away. "I didn't want to remember that. Why did you make me bring it all up?"

Kai said nothing, only holding me tighter as if his touch could soothe the pain away.

"I still have nightmares from that night," I admitted, my voice trembling. "I remember how he grabbed me and wouldn't let go. No matter how hard I tried, I couldn't fight him off. I can still feel how helpless I was, how he pinned me down like I was nothing."

Tears poured from my eyes again, hot and unrelenting. "You know what? Maybe it isn't kind of me to say this, but I didn't feel an ounce of sympathy when Dannie wrung the last breath out of his neck."

"I don't know what else to say," Kai whispered, his voice rough with emotion.

"You need to trust me."

"I do trust you."

"Then why don't you act like it? Do you know no one has ever trusted me? My family never believed I could accomplish anything on my own. My best friend couldn't trust me with her secrets. And now you don't trust that I wouldn't cheat on you?"

"That's not what I mean. I trust you, of course I do."

"Come with me."

Without another word, I grabbed his hand and pulled him out of the restaurant. I hailed a taxi, dragging him inside before Wendy and Trevon had a chance to catch up. I gave the driver the name of our hotel, determined to leave everything else behind us for now.

"What are you doing?"

"Introducing you to Dannie. You'll see. He's nice."

"I'm sorry for doubting you. I really am. You have no idea how much I hate myself right now."

I couldn't see his expression clearly in the dark, but under the streetlight, I could just make out the tension in his jaw. He wasn't happy.

"It wasn't your fault," I said quietly.

"Yes, but I had to go poking at that wound of yours. Believe me, I know about covering up old scars and never wanting to see them again."

"What kind of old scars?" I asked. I had always known that Kai wasn't as strong and charming as he pretended to be. Beneath the polished exterior, there were secrets he guarded fiercely—memories that haunted him, truths he refused to admit.

He hesitated. "When I—"

We pulled up to the hotel just as he was about to reveal his deepest, darkest secret. My heart pounded with anticipation, but the moment slipped away. At the entrance, a familiar figure stood beneath the warm golden lights, a cigarette glowing between his fingers.

"Hey, Dannie," I greeted him nonchalantly as I got out of the taxi.

Kai paid the driver and stepped out from other side, his posture tense but composed.

Dannie exhaled a slow stream of smoke, his sharp eyes narrowing slightly. "Where have you been? I had people looking for you everywhere."

Behind him, two men hovered just out of the light, their presence a quiet reminder of the world Dannie lived in. As Kai joined me, their steps grew heavier, edging closer.

"There's someone I want you to meet," I said, trying to ease the tension simmering in the air. "Kai, this is Dannie. Dannie, Kai."

I didn't want to define either man's role in my life. Labels would only complicate things further. Kai and I weren't officially anything, and Dannie didn't need to know the tangled history between us. Besides, which label should I choose for Dannie—my ex, my savior, my husband?

"Sorry for disappearing," I added, leaning against Kai. His hand found my waist, steady and reassuring. "I went out to find this one."

"Perfect timing," Dannie said, extending a hand toward me. "It's time for cake."

I straightened, pulling away from Kai's warmth. "What is going on?"

"It's my grandmother's birthday, remember? We're having a party upstairs," Dannie explained, his voice unusually light. He said it like I'd forgotten—but I was there. What was he really trying to say?

"You should go," Kai murmured, making a subtle gesture for me to leave.

I hesitated, leaning closer to whisper, "Thanks Kai."

"You should join us," Dannie added, surprising me with his invitation.

I smiled at Dannie, grateful for the effort he was making. With Kai by my side and Dannie leading the way, we entered the grand lobby and stepped into the elevator. Strangely, Dannie allowed his men to follow us inside. Normally, he preferred distance. Was it Kai's presence that changed his mind?

In the ballroom, the soft hum of conversation mixed with clinking glasses. Dannie gestured to a passing waitress to bring us some drinks. Both Kai and Dannie took a glass of champagne while I opted for sparkling water.

Kai studied Dannie for a moment. "You look familiar. Have we met before?"

Dannie gave a faint smile. "Maybe in a past life. But I do have one of those faces."

Dannie didn't. His face was the kind people remembered—the kind that made strangers look twice. Some wouldn't call him traditionally handsome, especially if they preferred clean-cut, Wall Street types. But his angular jaw, tall nose, and the mystery behind his gaze made him unforgettable. There was an exotic quality to him that kept people guessing about him. Was he Mongolian? Russian, perhaps?

"I'm usually very good with faces. Apologies if I've forgotten," Kai said smoothly.

"Not at all. I hear you're in the food business," Dannie replied. I felt the tension ripple inside me as I knew that he had a habit of keeping tabs on potential threats, but I hadn't realized that included Kai.

"Yes, among other things. Have you been to any of my restaurants?"

"Ding Lou was a favorite," Dannie admitted. "You're brave to open in Hong Kong."

The hair on my back prickled. Was that a warning? Without thinking, I reached out and tugged Dannie's sleeve lightly.

His expression softened instantly.

"What is it, sweetie? Are you okay?" His voice dipped gently, his gaze softer.

I shook my head quickly. "I'm fine."

Kai, however, wasn't letting it go. "What do you mean by brave?"

Dannie shrugged, his smile easy. "Hong Kongers have peculiar tastes. Everyone here thinks they're a food critic. I admire anyone bold enough to open a restaurant here, let alone succeed at it."

Kai's lips curled into a faint smile. "Thanks."

I exhaled softly, relieved by shift in tones. As the conversation moved to food and business, I watched them both carefully. I had expected this meeting to be tense, awkward even. But instead, the two men mingled effortlessly, as though they had known each other for years.

Laura leaned toward me excitedly. "Hey, I've been looking everywhere for you."

"Do you need help with something?" I asked, raising an eyebrow.

Laura wore a deep purple A-line dress that hugged her figure perfectly, making her look sweet and effortlessly adorable. The soft fabric accentuated her sharp dimples, brightened her already sparkling eyes, and made her teeth gleam like pearls. A good dress could elevate beauty—and on Laura, it worked like magic.

"I was going to introduce you to my best friend, but she already left," she said, a hint of disappointment lacing her voice.

"Why aren't you with Grandma?" Dannie asked. It might have sounded like a simple question to anyone else, but I knew exactly what it meant for Laura.

I felt the same when my parents asked why I was home instead of looking after someone they had sent to me. Like I'd failed them simply for taking a moment to breathe.

"Grandma's probably busy entertaining her guests," I answered quickly, standing up for Laura, wishing someone would do the same for me at work. Her arm, which was still hooked through mine, tensed slightly.

"I'm sure she is," Dannie said as he nodded.

Her gaze shifted. "Who's this?"

"I'm Kai," he said, extending his hand toward her. They shook hands firmly.

"Laura. Nice to meet you. Are you friends with my brother?"

"June invited him," Dannie cut in before I could answer, his tone cool and composed.

"Are you from the United States too?" Laura asked, curiosity flickering in her eyes.

"No, I'm from Shanghai," Kai replied smoothly.

"He's the owner of Ding Lou," Dannie added, offering the information before either of us could.

Laura's jaw dropped. "Oh my God, really? Grandma

and I love that restaurant! We, like, *have* to go there every single month. But it's so hard to get a reservation. Every time we dine there, we book our next visit months in advance!"

Her excitement was palpable, her cheeks flushed a delicate pink as she listed her favorite dish from the restaurant. Her skin glowed with a fresh, dewy finish, and her makeup was minimal—a refreshing contrast to the heavy glam most women wore at a party like this.

"You're invited to the headquarters in Shanghai anytime," Kai offered with a casual smile. "I'll have my head chef prepare something special for you."

I couldn't tell if Kai was serious, but Laura nearly trembled with excitement. If she were any younger, she might have jumped up and down in celebration.

As I watched the three of them interact, a strange feeling crept in. Maybe I'd been overreacting all along. Kai didn't seem bothered by Dannie's presence, despite him being my ex. And Dannie appeared completely unfazed by Kai being here as my "special friend".

"Please excuse me for a minute. I need to take care of some family business. Come with me, Laura," Dannie said, his tone leaving no room for argument.

I watched as he led Laura away, disappearing into the crowd. The party showed no signs of slowing down. Initially, I had assumed most of the guests were Dannie's friends and business associates, but it became clear they were here for his grandmother—many of them patiently waiting for a chance to speak with the matriarch.

Kai's voice pulled me back. His brows knitted closely,

like he was working through a puzzle. "I know him from somewhere. I just know it."

"Maybe at some party? Dannie has a lot of business connections."

"I wouldn't forget someone like him," he insisted. "Not with his reputation."

"Right," I murmured. "I told you he was nice."

"I can't believe he trusts you with me," he added quietly, his hand trailing up the small of my back.

"That he does. However, we must behave," I warned, stepping slightly away from his touch. "Some people here still think Dannie and I were married. Until he clears that up, we shouldn't risk embarrassing him at a party he's hosting for his grandmother."

"You're right," he agreed, though his lips pressed into a thin line.

We shifted our conversation to Dave—that Lincoln's team still couldn't find anything. Kai's expression darkened and he agreed that they might need to involve the Mafia, if they still had no luck.

Laura reappeared at her grandmother's request. Apparently, she wanted me to meet a few people. I excused myself from the conversation I was having and followed Laura toward the center of the hall.

Dannie's grandmother had moved from the dining table to a cushioned chair in the Mahjong area. There were about ten tables scattered across the section, though only three were fully occupied. As I approached, she caught sight of me and waved enthusiastically, gesturing for me to sit beside her. Dannie was already seated on her other side, his expression unreadable.

A line of people soon began to form in front of her, each one stepping forward in turn to offer their well-wishes. They greeted her with warm smiles and polite words, wishing her a happy birthday and many more years of health and happiness. After presenting their gifts, she reciprocated by handing each person a red envelope. Before they left, she took the time to introduce me to each guest. Dannie, of course, required no introduction—everyone at the party knew exactly who he was.

After the older guests had finished, the younger generation followed suit. They greeted her with birthday wishes, received a red envelope, and were then expected to address Dannie and me using titles she had assigned based on their relationship to us.

Some called me "sam sam," others "biu yi," "biu sou," "kao mou," and "yiyi." The only one I recognized was "yiyi," which sounded like "auntie" in Mandarin. As for the rest, I was clueless. My knowledge of the Chinese family tree was embarrassingly limited. Growing up, I had simply called any older man "uncle" and any older woman "auntie," which had always seemed to work just fine.

"You're very pretty," one of the younger girls said shyly, planting a soft kiss on my cheek after completing her greeting.

"Oh, you see? Children like you," Dannie's grandmother said with a delighted chuckle.

I smiled awkwardly, "I wasn't really doing anything."

"Exactly. You should have children of your own," she added with a pointed look that made my stomach twist with discomfort.

I shifted uneasily in my seat, silently pleading for this ordeal to end. Just then, in the blur of moving bodies, I caught a glimpse of Kai's face. It was fleeting—no more than two seconds—but enough to make my pulse quicken.

"Isn't it time for cake?" I blurted out, a little too eagerly.

Dannie, sensing my discomfort, sprang into action. He helped his grandmother rise from her chair while barking instructions to someone nearby, presumably about the cake. Relief flooded through me—finally, an escape from this never ending procession.

He guided his grandmother toward a small, elevated stage where an elaborate cake waited, its tiers adorned with delicate sugar flowers. As he helped her up the steps, he raised an eyebrow at me, silently urging me to follow.

"Do I need to?" I mouthed, hoping he'd let me off the hook.

"June, where are you?" His grandmother's voice cut through the noise, leaving me with no choice but to hurry to her side. She beamed as the photographer positioned us around the cake, and with Dannie on her other side, she cut the first slice while the camera flashed repeatedly.

Just when I thought the worst was over, she clapped her hands. "Family photo! Laura, gather everyone."

I barely suppressed a groan as Laura began herding people toward the stage. What followed was ten grueling minutes of endless photos. The first five shots were genuine family portraits. After that, it was a mix of random guests—some claiming distant ties to Dannie, while others were clearly just business associates. A few, from the looks of them, were probably triad members.

As we finally stepped off the stage, I leaned close to Dannie and whispered. "You owe me big time."

14

Kai

Dannie's grandmother wore an exquisite set of lavender jade jewelry: a necklace, earrings and a bracelet. The stones ranged from half an inch to a full inch in size. They might not have been the most expensive jewelry I had ever seen, but it must have cost a fortune to collect enough of those rare stones to craft such an elaborate set. And the purple jade she wore wasn't just any ordinary variety—it was the rare and coveted Di Wang purple jade, a shade once reserved for emperors. A true symbol of class and prestige.

The old lady had a kind face, or so it seemed. She smiled the entire time I was there. It wasn't a wide grin but a polite, measured smile—one that was anything but genuine. Everyone in the business world was familiar with such gestures. I, for one, had spent years perfecting a smile that could appear on demand, one that needed to be charming and not at all creepy. Trust me, it took practice.

There were days when faking a pleasant demeanor felt impossible, no matter what. And I had to hand it to the old lady—she was a master at delivering a flawless, effortless, and elegant fake smile.

It was one thing hearing about June's arrangement with Dannie.

Seeing it firsthand was an entirely different story.

If June hadn't confided in me, I would have assumed they were a real couple—just like every other person in this ballroom. And the calculating old lady made sure everyone knew that June was her granddaughter-in-law. She couldn't fool me with her sweet facade.

I'd seen this act before. Older people loved to meddle in their family's affairs when they should have just minded their own business. This woman, like my own mother, undoubtedly took pleasure in pulling strings.

The way she orchestrated the evening was no accident. She had people lining up, presenting themselves one by one, and she took the time to introduce June to each one of them personally. No one else was seated beside her—not even Laura, the woman who, from what I had overheard, had devoted most of her life to caring for the old woman.

Without making any formal announcement, she had cemented the image of June and Dannie as a couple. And in many ways, that silent declaration was far more personal and powerful.

I'd never cared about the background of the women I dated. Sure, my crew ran checks on everyone I encountered, but as long as their bad intentions weren't aimed at me, it didn't matter. Some of my dates had criminal records. Nothing too serious—petty theft at most—no bank robberies or mastermind-level scams.

But watching June being embraced by Dannie's family, friends, and dubious associates, I couldn't help but wonder: how big of a favor had she done for Dannie? Did she fully understand what she was getting herself into? And more importantly, would this favor ever truly end?

I expected them to finish the introductions and move on to cutting cake. I was wrong. More people waited to meet her. I knew what this meant in the business world. These people were seizing the opportunity to become more than mere acquaintances—to pave the way for future opportunities.

Jealousy coiled inside me, dark and relentless. I couldn't see how June could ever escape being Mrs. Wu. Even if we eloped and married in Vegas., these people would always see her as *his* wife. She could never truly be mine.

Jenny needed me.

June needed my trust.

I reminded myself that I was only one person.

There was nothing I could do about June. I had promised to trust her, and I needed to hold up my end of the bargain—even if it tore me apart inside.

I texted Trevon, updating him on how June and I had run into Dannie and how I had ended up in the very room we had tried, and failed, to get into earlier.

Trevon decided not to push his luck again. Those

men wouldn't forget a big Black man attempting to crash their exclusive party—not in a city where people who looked like him were a minority.

Another text let me know that he and Wendy were hanging out in the lobby with Clare.

Clare. Of course. I hadn't forgotten about her or her mistake. I wasn't deliberately trying to punish her, but I couldn't spare the energy to manage her while everything else spiraled around me. She was probably panicking, terrified of losing a job that overpaid her for doing very little. As long as she stayed out of my way and didn't piss me off, she would keep that job.

I wondered if Trevon would even be allowed through the door if Wendy vouched for him. Then again, they probably didn't care enough about Wendy to let her bring a guest.

A part of me died each time June shook another hand. With every introduction, another person in that room became a witness to the lie that she and I didn't belong together. I watched her from behind a wall of people, feeling like a pathetic loser. Occasionally, her gaze found mine. She would offer a subtle reassurance— a nod, a small smile, a fleeting gesture. Each one was a lifeline, a spark that made me crave her even more.

She gave me something no one else ever could: recognition. A sense of belonging. An energy that felt like a magic pill, easing the growing fear that I wasn't enough.

For years, I had battled the anxiety that seized me whenever danger crept too close. Dave had learned to anticipate my triggers, eliminating threats before they could affect me. And if he couldn't prevent them, he would warn me, preparing me for the worst.

I had tried everything to cure the anxiety that haunted me—the sudden, unpredictable breakdowns that paralyzed me at the slightest hint of danger. My training in multiple martial arts, hoping that constant exposure to practice and controlled attacks would numb me to the fear. But it never worked.

Extreme sports were the other thing I tried. The adrenaline rush from car racing, rock climbing, and skydiving had never triggered an episode. But lately, something had changed.

And I was sure it had everything to do with June.

If it weren't for her, my body would have shut down completely, and it would have taken me hours or even days to recover from the sight of someone being held at gunpoint. But instead of collapsing into a useless pile of flesh when Jenny went missing, I stood up and took matters into my own hands. I had accomplished many things in life, but year after year, I failed to battle my own demons—until now. Until June came back into my life.

I needed June.

"Hey, mind if I join you?" Laura's voice cut through my thoughts as she stood next to the empty chair across from me.

"Sure," I said, pulling the chair out for her.

"Are you hungry?" she asked. I shook my head, but she had already flagged down a waitress, ordering a selection of cakes.

"Thanks," I muttered. I didn't want cake, but she probably did, and I knew better than to question her.

"No problem. There are three flavors. You'll see," she said with a smile, and I gave a noncommittal nod, unwilling to muster another thank you.

The waitress returned with two large plates, each holding three rectangular slices of cake in varying shades of brown, yellow and green. Laura's lips—a deep shade of adzuki bean red—curled into a smile, revealing her pearly white teeth.

"I love cake," she declared brightly.

"I figured," I replied, the smile on her paper-white face making her fondness obvious.

"How do you know June?" she asked, cutting into one of the slices.

"Me?" I echoed. She nodded, her mouth too full of cake to speak. "Through my friend—her brother."

"She has a brother?" She asked once she swallowed.

"Two, actually."

She hummed in approval as she sampled another bite.

"Chocolate with goji berry," she announced, her fork already spearing the next bite. "It was an interesting combination I hadn't tried before."

"That good, huh?" I asked, watching her reaction.

She bobbled her head enthusiastically. "Do you have any siblings?"

"Yes."

"Are you close?"

"No."

"Oh."

I realized too late that my bluntness had killed the conversation. Worse still, it reminded me how much

Dannie and I had in common. For one, we both wanted the same woman. And neither of us was close to our siblings.

I hadn't even known about my half-brother until I was a young adult—a revelation delivered through a phone call with my mother, her voice raw with rage. He was someone born to steal everything I had, to replace me before I even knew he existed.

Growing up, I had wanted a brother to play with. Jenny had no interest in the kind of games I wanted to play. Once, she forced me to participate in her make-believe fashion show. She dressed me in her homemade designs, which involved adding bright colors to her mother's pristine, ten-thousand-thread-count Egyptian sheets. We both earned a spanking from our mothers that night. After that, I never played dress-up with her again.

"So, you didn't have anyone to play with growing up?" Laura asked, her voice soft with curiosity.

"I did, briefly."

"A cousin? A friend?"

"A friend," I admitted, thinking of the one I had before my kidnapping.

She moved on to the butter-colored slice of cake and offered another comment. "Vanilla. Such a classic."

"How about you?" I asked, sensing the conversation drifting toward an awkward silence. She had made an effort to keep me company—the least I could do was return the gesture and pretend to care about her seemingly perfect life.

"I don't have friends," she said bluntly.

"Really?" I should have left it there, but the words

slipped out. "For a nice girl like you? I find that hard to believe."

Her face softened. "You think I'm nice?"

Did I? We had only just met. I didn't know why she had chosen to sit with me, why she was filling the air with pointless conversation. Maybe Dannie sent her to fish for information, but if that was the case, she was terrible at her job.

Sometimes, you could just sense things about people. Laura seemed a little lost in life.

Dannie on the other hand, was one of those unreadable types, the kind you could never quite figure out.

"Yes," I finally said, giving her the answer she wanted to hear.

"I guess you're right," she murmured, setting down her fork and leaving the last piece of cake untouched. "Everyone thinks I'm nice. All my so-called friends. They use me to get places, pay for things, scare off guys who bother them."

"I understand," I said quietly.

Her eyes searched my face, as if trying to determine if I truly meant it. "You do?"

"Yes."

The young woman studied me a moment longer before leaning back in her chair. "How do you get rid of people like that?"

"Learn to say no."

"Nonononono," she said quickly, dragging out the word. "Like this?"

"Not quite. You need to say it like you mean it."

"No!" she said louder this time, her voice ringing with more conviction.

"Like it would cost you an arm."

"NO!" Her voice echoed through the room, drawing a few curious glances. She clapped a hand over her mouth, her cheeks turning the shade of a ripe tomato.

"That's more like it," I said, unable to suppress a small smile.

"That was kind of fun," she giggled, her laughter light and musical. "What about your family? Have you ever said no to them?"

She picked up her fork again and finished off the last bite of cake.

"Depends on who we're talking about," I admitted. I had always let my mother walk all over me, too afraid to break her heart after my father left.

I angled my head slightly, trying to get a better view of what June was up to. But there was no sign of her—I suspected the old lady hadn't finished showing her off to her peers.

"I couldn't say no to my family," I said quietly.

"Don't feel bad about that. I'm guessing half of the people in this world have the same issue," she replied. "Except, I'm actually an orphan. My family... they aren't my real family."

I wasn't expecting that. She must have had quite a bit to drink tonight to open up to me like that.

"Can I share something with you?" I asked, lowering my voice.

"What?" She leaned closer, her eyes glinting with curiosity. "You can tell me."

"My father abandoned us for a different family."

Her face softened. "Oh no, I'm sorry."

These days, it wasn't much of a secret. He had been seen in public with his mistress and their son, as if we had never existed.

"Are they nice to you? Your adopted family?" I asked, steering the conversation back to her.

"Grandmother is nice. And Dannie? Oh well, he's just cold. I guess with our age gap, we never really had much in common to talk about."

"There are two sides to a coin. Is one side better than the other?" It was something clever I had read in a Zen book once, though I couldn't quite remember how the rest of it went.

Her posture straightened slightly, anticipation flickering across her face as she waited for me to elaborate. I searched my mind, but nothing else came.

"Maybe. Maybe not," she said finally, her tone thoughtful.

"If only the world were as clear as black and white," I murmured, letting my words trail off, aware that I had once again failed to sound profound.

She was young, with her whole life ahead of her. Whatever wisdom I thought I had couldn't possibly prepare her for the road she needed to walk herself. Our lives were too different. I couldn't live hers, and she couldn't live mine. What worked for me might not work for her.

"You'll figure it out in your own time," I added softly.

"Persimmon."

I blinked, frowning at her sudden declaration. "What?"

She pointed at her mouth. "The last cake. It's persimmon."

"Right. The cake."

"Never would have guessed. I thought it might be orange or peach, judging by the color. Isn't life just full of surprises?" She smiled to herself, as if the realization had unlocked something deeper.

I nodded, even though I knew she wasn't really asking for my opinion. She had just experienced a lightbulb moment.

I'd had a lightbulb moment of my own.

It made sense now why she seemed so detached when they gathered for a family photo earlier. She didn't feel like she belonged.

"Do you need a drink?" I asked, feeling the weight of my thoughts pressing heavier by the second. Soon, I would have to leave and face the music—leave June with Dannie while I handled the chaos brewing in Shanghai. I shook my head, but the image of Chen Gong, covered in blood, refused to fade. I needed something stronger to push it away.

"Not really. Are you going to eat that?" Laura nodded toward my untouched cake, her eyes gleaming with mischief.

"No. Knock yourself out."

I slipped away toward the bar, which was tucked inside a smaller room near the ballroom entrance. It was quieter here—a welcome contrast to the noise outside.

There was only one bartender and a lone patron: a woman slumped over the counter, her face buried in the crook of her arms.

"Can I get a whiskey, please?"

"Of course, sir."

"How much do I owe you?"

"It's free of charge. Drink as much as you like," the woman sat up, giggled as she replied quickly, supporting her chin with her palm.

"Thank you," I said, accepting the glass of golden liquid. It burned in all the right places as I took a sip.

I turned to head back to the ballroom. As much as I welcomed the calm in here, a part of me felt the need to keep an eye on June while I still could. My rational brain told me she was safe—surrounded by people who adored her. But instinct told me otherwise.

A loud thud shattered the quiet.

I spun around to find the woman collapsed on the floor, limbs sprawled awkwardly.

The bartender and I rushed to her side. She wasn't heavy, but with so much alcohol in her, she was nothing more than dead weight. We carried her to a small armchair against the wall. Once she was secure, the bartender returned to his station to fetch her a glass of water, leaving me alone with her.

"Leng chai..."

The words pierced through the haze of alcohol. It meant 'handsome man' in Cantonese. But in a different tone, it could also mean 'child'. The voice was dense and low, damaged by years of smoking.

A voice I hadn't heard in years.

My chest tightened.

"Auntie Five," I whispered.

The woman who had been behind my kidnapping.

15

Kai

"Hey lady," I shook the unconscious woman in front of me, but nothing happened. I tried again, more vigorously this time, shaking her with both hands. Apart from a lopsided twitch of her mouth, there was no other reaction.

"Do you know who she is?" I asked the skinny redheaded bartender hovering nearby.

"She's a guest, of course. No one gets in unless they're invited." He set a glass of water on the coffee table beside the armchair.

She wasn't going to drink that water—not if she remained unconscious, oblivious to the world around her. I briefly considered throwing it on her. Maybe that would wake her up faster.

Auntie Five. I hadn't seen her for over twenty years, but despite the faint lines etched into her face, she hadn't changed much. Her hair was as dark and glossy as I remembered, clearly dyed and maintained by a professional. Most women her age put on more weight than they'd like, but she hadn't. Still, time hadn't been kind to her. She had to be around my mother's age, yet she looked ten—maybe fifteen—years older.

"Can you get me another whiskey?" I held out my hand to the redhead for a handshake. It was an odd gesture for an order, but he took it, surprise flickering across his face as he found the cash I had discreetly tucked into his palm.

"Anything else I can get for you, sir?" He grinned, eager now.

"Her name."

"I'll be right back." The young man disappeared through a door behind the bar.

I studied her from head to toe. She was dressed like a celebrity attending the Oscars—impeccably styled and undoubtedly expensive. I couldn't pinpoint the designer, but I had shopped enough to recognize high-end craftmanship. Her jewelry was understated—a few simple diamond pieces—but the cut and clarity suggested they were far from cheap.

She was doing well for herself.

Was any of her lifestyle funded by me? By the ransom from kidnapping a young boy?

Calm down, I warned myself. There was no proof she had anything to do with it. If she had, the police would have charged her back then. But my mother had been convinced Auntie Five was involved.

Can't trust her.

The thought slithered through my mind. But who couldn't I trust—this woman, or my mother?

"That's Ms. Wu," the waiter said, returning with my whiskey. "She comes to these parties all the time—always drinks until she blacks out."

"You didn't already know that she's a regular?"

"Nah, I just started last week. Dropped out of college." He shrugged.

"You don't work for... the host?" I lowered my voice, unwilling to say Dannie's name aloud.

"Mr. Wu? Yes and no. I work for the hotel, not him."

"Doesn't he own the hotel?"

"I heard he part-owns it. Apparently, his partner runs the day-to-day stuff."

That made sense. Someone like Dannie—head of a criminal organization—wouldn't waste time managing a hotel.

"What else do you know about her?" I pressed. As much as I wanted intel on Dannie, this kid wasn't the person to ask.

He hesitated, then said, "I asked around, but no one really knows who she is. Just that she's important, and no one ever stops her from coming in. My only job is to give her whatever she wants to keep her happy."

"Thanks."

"Anything else, sir?"

"No."

Ms. Wu.

Now I remembered why I called her Auntie Five. Her surname, Wu, sounded like the number five in Chinese.

When I was a kid, the adults laughed and loved the nickname I'd given her.

Who was she to Dannie? Were they related?

I briefly considered offering the bartender a side gig—spying on Auntie Five and Dannie for me—but dismissed the idea. I knew nothing about him. Without Dave to run a background check, I was flying blind. I had to find a way to bring Dave back, no matter what.

The young man returned to his post behind the bar. I opened the woman's handbag and pulled out her phone. It was locked. I patted her face gently and held the device up to her. A faint click let me know the phone had unlocked.

Auntie Five slumped back, her eyes fluttering shut again, utterly unconcerned about what I was doing. I dialed the burner phone Trevon had given me, ensuring I had her number saved for future use. If Dave—or even Clare—were here, they'd already be digging up everything there was to know about her.

I had no proof that her phone number would help me place her later, but I knew one thing: she had status here. Enough to come and go as she pleased.

"Who are you?" Her voice was hoarse as she propped herself up on the side of the chair, blinking rapidly like the dim lighting hurt her eyes.

"Ms. Wu, are you okay? You fainted."

"I fainted?" Fainted, passed out—same thing when you drank yourself into oblivion.

"Yes, I found you collapsed over there." I pointed toward the spot where she'd been sprawled. A flash of Chen Gong's lifeless body surged through my mind. I shook off the image, but a chilling question lingered—would this memory ever stop haunting me?

"Thank you, handsome. You're very kind. No one cares about me anymore."

A heavy sigh escaped her lips as she pulled out a few one-hundred-dollar bills and handed them to me. I pushed her hand away, my pride refusing to let me accept her money like this. I had plenty of my own—I certainly didn't need hers.

In the end, I waved the waiter over, handed him the cash, and instructed him to get her something hot. Tea, coffee, whatever he could find behind that brown door he had disappeared into earlier.

"What's my phone doing out here?" Now that she was more alert, I could see that life hadn't been kind to her. Her oddly plump face was a telltale sign of Botox, but beneath the artificial smoothness lingered something raw and real.

Sadness. And no plastic surgery in the world could ever erase that.

"I must have taken it out at some point then," she murmured, rummaging through her small black handbag.

I watched her in silence, noting the tremor in her hands as she checked the contents of her purse.

"Do you need me to take you to the hospital, Auntie Five?" My attempt to keep calling her Ms. Wu faltered as the old nickname slipped from my lips.

Her head lifted slightly, her expression unreadable.

"No, no need," she replied, her tone dismissive.

She didn't flinch at the name, but she did take her

time studying me. Her gaze wasn't harsh—not at all—but something about it made my stomach lurch.

"Well, if you're okay, then I should really get going." I turned and left without waiting for the young waiter to return.

But my mind wouldn't let her go. The questions that had haunted me for years resurfaced with a vengeance. Had she betrayed me back then? Sold my information to the kidnappers just to make a quick buck? Did she know what they did to me—how they punched and kicked a helpless boy who couldn't defend himself? Had she ordered it?

I had lived with those questions for so long. And now, here she was. I wanted answers.

If she tried to kidnap me again, it wouldn't be so easy this time. I could take her instead. Return the favor. Let her feel the terror of being captured and locked away in a small, dark, stinking room where no one came to save you.

But I couldn't risk her discovering who I really was. Not without Dave and Clare. Not in a room full of triad members. And not with June in such easy reach.

"Leng Chai," she called softly, but I pretended not to hear her.

I returned to the table where I had left Laura. June had found her way there and was now sitting beside her, chatting and giggling. More cakes had appeared—three extra plates piled high with more than two women could possibly eat.

Dannie slipped past me and claimed the seat next to June, and I swore he did it on purpose.

My mind was still tangled with thoughts of Auntie Five, warning me that this place was dangerous. These people weren't my friends. If they wanted to, they could lock me up again. Worse, they could take June, Trevon and Wendy too. We were foreigners, mere guests in Hong Kong. If the triad decided we were a problem, we could disappear without a trace—like those backpackers who were never heard from again.

The crowd had thinned, and I saw my chance. I leaned in close to June and whispered, "We should make a move. I have an early flight tomorrow."

"Okay," she agreed softly. "Let me quickly say goodbye to a few people."

I braced myself. Someone—Laura, Dannie or his grandmother—would surely try to make her stay.

But surprisingly, Dannie handed us a keycard.

"My personal suite," he said with a smirk.

I took the card without hesitation. Now wasn't the time for pride. One day, maybe I'd buy a hotel chain and have my own personal suite in every city around the world. But right now, all I wanted was to get out of there.

I shouldn't have left Jenny behind. Alone and helpless. The mess was partly my fault, and I had abandoned her to clean it up.

Tomorrow, I had to leave. No matter what.

As we prepared to go, June stopped to speak with the man who had promised to help her with the visa tomorrow. She wanted to confirm the time and the documents she needed to bring.

I told her she could take her time sorting out the visa

now that we'd finally seen each other. But she insisted on coming to Shanghai to join me as soon as possible.

Part of me was touched by her compassion, her love, and her affection for me. The other part was filled with worry—worried that she might have to witness what awaited me in Shanghai: the mess, the criminal charges, the horror.

I used the moment to call Trevon and update him. I also had Clare organize a few things for me. Her voice trembled with emotion—as if she'd been waiting desperately for an assignment. I reminded myself not to let my guard down again. Getting too close to my bodyguard could lead to complications.

Leaving the room with June felt strange. I was used to being watched wherever I went, but this was different. It felt wrong, somehow. The stares followed us like we were doing something criminal.

"Is it me, or is everyone staring?" June whispered.

"Yes, they are," I confirmed.

"Great. Let them stare," she said with a wink.

That wink was trouble. It held the same teasing spark she had the night of the gala, when she asked if I wanted to claim our first date. Just the memory of that night had my dick hard.

I let out a low, restrained groan in response.

We were still walking apart from each other—about a foot too far. June wanted to respect whatever agreement she had with Dannie. I adored her for that. But her promise to him was killing me inside. The urge to reach for her waist and pull her into my arms was almost unbearable.

We waited outside the elevator with several other people. It seemed like everyone had decided to leave at the same time. A woman in her forties started studying me closely, her eyes widening in sudden recognition.

"Li Kai?" she gasped, as if she had just pieced together who I was. I nodded and offered her a polite smile. The murmur spread like wildfire. A few others turned to stare, whispering among themselves. Some tried to be discreet, but not discreet enough—I could hear their hushed conversations.

I sighed quietly, frustration simmering beneath the surface. This was the kind of bullshit I dealt with daily. The only blessing about this trip was that the paparazzi hadn't caught wind of my visit. Yet. And in Hong Kong, they were the worst kind imaginable—relentless and merciless.

A soft brush against the side of my hand snapped me out of my thoughts. The unexpected contact sent a jolt of electricity down my spine. I turned my head slightly, nodding at the nosy onlookers and signaling they could take the elevator first. June's fingers were growing bolder, brushing mine again. A quiet rebellion in a crowded space.

An elevator heading up finally arrived, and June stepped inside with a perfectly straight face. I followed, giving a brief wave to the gawking strangers still waiting for the one going down.

The moment the doors slid shut, June grabbed my face and pulled me into a kiss. Her mouth was hot, wet and sweet—so damn sweet. I couldn't get enough of that taste, the taste that was uniquely hers. I kissed her back, hard, savoring every second, every flick of her tongue.

My hand slid to the back of her head, fingers tangling in her silky hair as I tugged her closer. I needed more. My cock throbbed in protest, straining against my pants, aching for the touch I craved. She stumbled slightly, her legs weakening as she backed into the mirrored wall.

"Are you okay?" I murmured, though my voice was rough with desire.

She didn't answer with words. Instead, she grabbed my tie and yanked me against her. Our bodies collided, and when our hips met, the heat between us burning hotter. It was as if our bodies recognized each other, missed each other—no matter how much time had passed.

I wanted to take her right then and there. Right against the elevator wall. But reality had other plans. The elevator dinged, the doors sliding open, mocking the perfect plan that had been forming in my head. There was never enough time during an elevator ride, no matter how much the movies romanticized it. We could have pressed the emergency button, but I knew it wouldn't be enough. Not for what I wanted.

Grunting in frustration, I lifted her into my arms, cradling her like the princess she was. It didn't take us long to find Dannie's personal suite. There were only two rooms on this floor—one on the right, one on the left. His was the right one. Fitting for someone like him. Always had to be right.

"Right front pocket," I told her, shifting her weight

slightly to keep her comfortable. That was where I had tucked the keycard.

Still wrapped in my arms, she reached down my pants pocket to retrieve it. It wasn't easy. I had to adjust a few times to give her better access. Her fingers brushed against my cock in the process, sending a fresh surge of arousal through me. I groaned softly, my body reacting instantly to her touch.

"Found it," she said, her voice teasing as she pulled the keycard free and waved it in front of me.

She giggled, clearly enjoying herself, but the real fun hadn't even begun. I wasn't about to put her down. Not when I wanted to hold her as close as possible before I had to leave her again. And keeping her in my arms meant she couldn't run away from me either.

After a few breathless seconds, she swiped the card on the reader and pulled the handle. As soon as the door clicked open, she wrapped her arms around my neck and kissed me again, fierce and unrestrained.

Lust. Desire. Hunger.

I could taste it in her mouth. Sweet and sinful. Her lips moved against mine with a kind of desperation, a need that mirrored my own. She moaned softly as I deepened the kiss, our mouths tangling in a feverish dance.

I pushed the door open with my back, scanning the room for the nearest surface. My dick throbbed painfully, and I knew I couldn't wait much longer. There was no bed in sight. Unlike the standard room Trevon had gotten us earlier, this suite had multiple rooms. But I didn't need a bed.

I needed a wall, a table—something. Anything to give us what we both wanted so desperately.

16

Kai

In the end, I settled on a three-seater couch positioned in front of what looked like a 77-inch TV. Behind the sofa stretched a floor-to-ceiling window, showcasing the city skyline.

I sat down, June still in my arms.

That was when she came alive.

She kissed my cheek—left, then right. Her lips trailed up to my right eye. I leaned back, moaning softly, closing my eyes, savoring the delicate pleasure of her kisses.

Forehead. Left eye. Left earlobe. Neck.

June was kissing me.

Not Dannie—whatever his name was. He was irrelevant right now. She had chosen me. Not him.

The competitive side of me couldn't help but pat myself on the shoulder, congratulating the less confident part of me for winning June.

No air in my lungs.

I couldn't breathe the more she kissed me.

No words in my mouth. Except her name.

I moaned her name. I wanted to tell her how much she meant to me, but nothing came out. I had always known what to say to a woman in bed. It was second nature to me. I always knew what to say, how to let a woman know they were beautiful, they were sexy. But right now? Nothing.

She was more than everything I had ever known.

So fucking beautiful.

So damn sexy.

Young me wouldn't have survived a woman like her. She wasn't the most gorgeous woman in the world—not even the most gorgeous woman I had been with.

But she was my dream woman.

Given time, any man could grow bored of the most stunning woman. But their dream woman? Never.

I sat there, mind completely blank. I was hers, completely hers. Whatever she wanted to do to me, whatever she wanted me to do to her.

Then the kisses stopped.

Or the nibbling.

Either way, my left earlobe wasn't happy.

She sat up, one leg draped over mine before straddling my lap. With deliberate control, she lifted my chin with the tip of her finger, hunching over to press her lips to mine.

Breath left my lungs.

I cupped the back of her head, my mouth searching for air in hers.

Desperate.

My life depended on it.

She parted her lips further. Our tongues met.

Then came the explosion—hot, wet, messy. A storm of passion that went on for what felt like forever. Even if I wanted to stop, I couldn't. Her mouth, her tongue, her scent, her taste—everything about her was so addictive. I wanted more. I needed more.

Greedy.

Like a starving puppy that could never be full.

My hands slid over her body, her skin radiating heat, an undeniable lust seeping between us, urging our bodies to connect.

Like two lost puzzle pieces that fit together perfectly.

Cliche, but true.

She moaned, the vibrations travelling through my mouth, up my brain, down my spine, and straight to my dick.

It was a signal.

My princess.

The woman of my dreams.

A moan escaped my throat in response to her call.

"I miss you."

Words. Finally.

She ran her fingers through my hair and smiled.

"Unbutton me."

I groaned in reply.

There was no zipper on her dress. Just three paokou buttons at the front. June arched back as I worked on the first one at her collar. It came undone quickly.

The second one wasn't as cooperative. Who the hell

designed these buttons? They were intricate, beautiful—but a nightmare to undo.

"Rip it."

My cock hardened instantly.

I loved this side of her, the side that took control, commanded me.

Pop. Pop. I tore them apart as she commanded.

Her nipples strained against the thin, silky fabric of her dress. Damn these Chinese dresses—beautiful, elegant, but frustratingly obstructive.

I couldn't wait.

I cupped her breasts, pressing my lips to the left, then to the right. I breathed in her scent—perfume, warmth, desire—and sucked.

Lick. Suck. Bite. Breathe.

My mouth busied itself as my hands pulled the dress over her head.

Then again—lick, suck, bite.

This time, without the fabric.

I dragged my tongue around her nipple, teasing, savoring. She arched back, her skin flushed, her breath uneven. Her nipple—red, the color of a kidney bean, and just as firm as an uncooked one.

So fucking sexy.

I held her close but not too tight.

I had always believed she was mine, that she would wait for me. That I just needed to be ready to sweep her off her feet.

Until I saw Dannie.

Until I saw the way he looked at her.

He saw her. Really saw her. The same way I did.

He saw what made her perfect, what made her a dream woman. And he wasn't afraid to claim her.

He didn't wait.

"Princess, baby," I whispered, a sliver of insecurity creeping into my voice.

"Yes?" She played with my hair.

"Are you really here?"

"Of course." She leaned in, her nose brushing against mine.

"It killed me, seeing you with him."

"I'm..." She cupped my face, "sorry," she murmured, pressing a kiss to my lips. "I thought it was a harmless favor," she whispered against my skin, kissing my eye, "until I saw how sad you were."

Our lips met again, a slow, unyielding collision of longing and desperation.

I wanted her.

Needed her. And I had to show her just how much.

I'd waited my entire life for her. Waited for the right time, for myself to be ready. But the last few hours had been the worst. The longest. The hardest. The most agonizing wait of my existence.

Now that she was finally mine, I couldn't let go.

But tomorrow, I would have to leave her.

I wanted to stay.

Staying was easy.

Leaving was impossible.

But when had doing the impossible ever been a choice?

The night was still young, but dawn would come too soon, stealing her from me before I was ready.

I flipped June over, her bare skin pressing against the plush brown suede of the couch. Her breath hitched as she instinctively moved to cover herself—one hand over the center of her chest, the other hovering near her core.

"Don't," I murmured, gently grasping her wrists and easing them away, exposing her fully to my gaze.

"Then stop looking at me like that," she whispered, voice trembling.

"Like what?"

"Like I'm the only thing you see."

I leaned in, my lips brushing the nape of her neck before trailing lower. A kiss against her collarbone. Another between the valley of her breasts. A slow, reverent path down her torso—upper abs, middle, lower.

Her thighs parted.

Wide.

I pressed my lips to the delicate crest of her V.

Her scent—God, her scent. The warm, intoxicating musk that curled around my senses, undoing every last shred of control I had left.

I didn't need to look to know she was soaked with anticipation.

How could I make her wait any longer?

I stuck my tongue out and licked.

She moaned.

That was the green light.

I licked again, this time savoring the taste that was uniquely hers—warm, intoxicating, utterly addictive.

"You're so ready for me," I murmured, my breath hot against her.

My tongue flicked over her clit, teasing, as my fingers

trailed along the seam of her slick entrance before sliding inside. One finger. Then another. Parting her, stretching her.

"Oh God," she groaned, her voice a broken whisper as my tongue circled her clit, my fingers curling, stroking that perfect spot deep inside her.

The fire in her eyes nearly undid me. I wanted to take her right then, to sink inside her and claim every inch of her. But then it would be over too quickly.

I wanted to savor her.

So I licked her again, drinking in the sweetness of her arousal. There was something almost creamy about it—like almond milk with a hint of something purely her. My lips wrapped around her clit as my fingers moved harder, faster, coaxing her closer to the edge.

Her hips jerked, instinctively moving against me, but she hesitated. She was holding back.

With one hand gripping her ass, I guided her forward, pressing her against my mouth. This was a dance, and she needed a lead.

And then she started responding.

Her breathing turned ragged, shallow yet desperate, every exhale laced with soft, breathy moans.

She tangled her fingers in my hair, tugging, pressing me closer, her movement shifting from hesitant to demanding. She rocked against my face, testing, teasing, chasing that high.

My cock throbbed inside my pants, aching for the attention my mouth was receiving. But this moment belonged to her.

I followed her lead, matching the rhythm she set, tongue and fingers working in perfect harmony.

She was in control.

I was merely here to worship her.

"Kai—oh God—" she growled, voice raw with pleasure. "What are you doing to me?"

She was close. So close.

I thrust my fingers deeper, faster, curling them just right, while my other hand gripped her ass, keeping her right where I wanted her.

Then, with a deep inhale, I sealed my mouth over her and devoured her, sucking every drop of her arousal as if it were the only thing keeping me alive.

And then—

She shattered.

A cry tore from her lips, her entire body trembling as waves of pleasure crashed over her.

It was the most beautiful sound I had ever heard—raw, erotic, utterly intoxicating. No song, no melody in the world could compare.

I pressed a kiss to her forehead as she collapsed against the couch, breathless, shaking.

She was quiet for a moment. Then, in a hesitant whisper, she asked, "Was it... disgusting? My taste?"

I frowned, lifting her chin, but she turned her head away, refusing to meet my gaze.

"This is not your first time?" I asked softly, curiosity swirling in my mind. What made her ask that? Had I done something wrong? I had tasted her before and I knew June wasn't a virgin.

She shook her head, avoiding my gaze. "I just... wasn't sure I tasted good."

"Oh, sweetheart." I brushed my lips over her temple. "You taste like heaven."

She threw a skeptical look at me, her eyes searching mine.

It hit me then—words weren't enough.

What did heaven taste like?

I exhaled, shaking my head with a grin. "It's hard to explain. Your scent, your taste—it drives me mad."

"Oh?"

"Yes. Can you not tell?"

She knew exactly what I meant. Her gaze flickered downward, a slow, knowing smile curving her lips.

Leaning on her side, she pushed herself up and began undressing me—tie, jacket, shirt, belt, pants, underwear—each piece peeled away with deliberate care. Her eyes never left mine.

Once I was bare before her, she rose to her feet and held out a hand. I took it, following her into the bedroom.

She sat at the edge of the super king bed, then slowly crawled backward toward the center. The invitation was clear.

I joined her, stretching out beside her, our bodies inches apart.

Just like that, we lay on our sides, facing each other. Minutes passed in silence. No words were needed.

Our gazes locked, deep and unbroken.

She traced her finger across my body. Gliding over my chest, pausing at my abs, as if she was memorizing every ridge and contour.

I mirrored her touch, running my fingers through her hair, then down her face, brushing along the curve of her neck.

Before I could trail lower, before my hand could reach the fullness of her breast, a sudden sensation stole my focus.

A sharp pulse.

A tingle.

A tightening ache that demanded attention.

My cock twitched, standing harder, stronger—aching for her touch.

We leaned in, our bodies molding together, legs tangled in a desperate embrace. My cock throbbed, content just to be near her—but greedy for more. Instinct took over, my hips shifting, the swollen head of my cock brushing against the slick entrance of her pussy.

Warm. Wet. Silken.

I reached down, sliding my fingers over her folds, feeling the perfect mix of her arousal and my own pre-cum. I teased her, rubbing slow, deliberate circles, massaging her with my hand and the tip of my dick.

She whined—a soft, melodic sound that shot straight through me.

My fingers worked her again and again, each touch more insistent, more demanding.

What the fuck was I doing? Torturing myself like this?

The longer I kept from sinking inside her, the more unbearable the need became.

My dick twitched, aching to thrust, to bury itself in the intoxicating heat between her thighs. I felt myself growing even harder, heavier—throbbing with an intensity I'd never experienced before. My dick had never been this fucking big. It strained, pulsed, and begged for her.

"I want you," she whispered, her voice sultry and breathless, like the star of an erotic film—not porn, but something more refined, more intoxicating.

The head of my cock lingered at her entrance, like a vampire waiting for an invitation. But those three words —soft and pleading—were all the permission I needed.

With deliberate care, I pushed forward, sinking into her inch by inch.

Her eyes fluttered shut. Her lips parted as she gasped for air, her body stretching to take me in.

Ah.

A groan rumbled from my chest as I clenched my eyes shut, overwhelmed by the sensation. The pressure, the tightness—fuck, it was almost too much.

I had the urge to laugh. Like a fucking giddy schoolboy having sex for the first time.

Of all the women I'd been with, none had never made me feel like this.

Her pussy fit around me like the perfect glove.

Custom-made. Designed just for me.

I pulled out.

Thrust back in.

Fuck, it felt incredible.

I kept moving, stroking deep, unable to stop. Unwilling to stop.

June moved with me, pressing closer, meeting every thrust with a need just as wild, just as desperate. Our lips crashed together, mouths searching, devouring—because even this, even sex, wasn't enough.

This wasn't just sex.

If it was, it wasn't anything like I remembered.

I wanted to stay inside her forever, wanted to keep her wrapped around me, melting into me. I drove deeper, making her cry out my name, and suddenly, something else flickered through me—something beyond pleasure, beyond lust.

I couldn't place it.

"Are you okay?" I murmured, kissed her forehead. "Does it hurt?"

She shook her head. I kissed her again—once, twice, three times—soft, lingering touches.

Her leg curled around my waist. My arms tightened around her, holding her close as we moved in perfect rhythm.

Side by side.

Bodies slick with sweat, clinging to each other like we'd fall apart if we let go.

Dancing a feverish, primal dance—one that neither of us wanted to end.

She shifted onto her side, and I followed, mirroring her movements. With effortless grace, she climbed over my thighs, settling on me. Our noses touched, breath mingling in the space between us. Then, as if drawn together by an invisible force, our mouths met again— hungry, searching, devouring.

And just like that, the lovemaking resumed.

She arched her back, supporting herself with one arm as she began to glide along my dick, her slick heat enveloping me inch by inch. My hands found her ass, cupping the soft flesh, kneading, guiding her rhythm as she rode me. The way she moved—grinding, circling, teasing—felt so fucking good, too good. A pleasure so intense it threatened to unravel me.

Not yet.

I clenched my jaw, losing control over the storm brewing inside me. I wouldn't let this end so soon. I couldn't.

Whatever this was between us, I had never felt anything like it before. And I never wanted it to end.

She leaned forward, wrapping one hand around my neck while the other pressed against my chest, tipping me back until I lay flat beneath her.

Her hair fell around us, strands brushing against my face like a whisper. Her body moved in fluid, hypnotic waves, her pussy gripping, and rubbing against my cock with slow, deliberate rhythm.

Then, she found it—the spot. I saw it in her eyes, a flicker of pleasure so raw it made my stomach tighten.

I groaned, capturing her nipple between my lips, sucking, teasing, rocking her hips against mine. My hands grasped her waist, guiding her, controlling the motion—pulling her down onto me, over and over, as she rode me harder.

Her weight, her grip, her warmth... It was everything.

I could do this all day.

From this angle, she was even more beautiful. I had fucked women before—many—but this was different. Something between us had changed.

For the first time in my life, I didn't crave my usual

vices. I didn't miss the toys, the mind games, the control. I didn't need to dominate her to stay hard. No twisted fantasies ran through my mind to keep me going.

Turned out, I wasn't the insatiable sex maniac I thought I was.

I had just been waiting for her.

She was close—I could feel it.

Her breath hitched, her body trembling above me. I rocked her harder, faster, helping her along the edge. She leaned back, grasping my hand in hers while her other hand cupped her breast. I thrust up into her from underneath, matching her rhythm, driving her higher, until—a sharp, broken cry spilled from her lips.

A sweet, melodic sound that sent me spiraling after her.

I came with her, lost in the moment, lost in her.

Her body collapsed against mine, warm and spent. I held her close, feeling the rise and fall of her breath, the damp heat of our skin pressed together.

Minutes passed in silence.

Then, a soft, barely audible sound reached my ears.

A snore.

I smirked, looking down at her sleeping form. June was out cold.

Carefully, I shifted, laying her down onto the pillow, pulling the blanket over her bare body. I watched her, listened to the quiet little noises she made in her sleep. Sometimes a murmur, sometimes nothing at all. A few times, she even mumbled words I couldn't quite make out.

At one point, I swore she said my name.

I wished I knew what she was dreaming about—whether it was something good, whether it was me.

Part of me wanted to wake her, to pull her on top of me and lose myself in her all over again. I didn't know if I'd ever feel that way again, if whatever had sparked this intensity between us would happen a second time.

Was it because I was leaving?

Was it the jealousy I had never felt before? The desperate, undeniable need to make her mine?

I didn't have the answers.

But I did know one thing.

I had no idea what was waiting for me in Shanghai.

Would I be charged for what happened to Chen? It was possible. I had watched him bleed to death. I could have called an ambulance, could have saved his life. But I didn't.

I sighed, glancing at the clock.

Time to move.

Time to man up.

Time to face my crime.

17

June

It was nice having Dannie wait for me at the building where the visa agency was located. Applying for a visa—or any official documents, for that matter—could be incredibly stressful. That had always been my experience. I would happily pay someone a small fee to handle the entire process on my behalf.

I hated the way the officers looked at people. Their judgmental eyes seemed to scan through your body, your brain, your bank account, your criminal record—leaving nothing hidden. I couldn't help but feel completely exposed in places like that. Airports, embassies, banks—those were the worst.

By the time I woke up, Kai had already left. This time, he had left a note on the pillow beside me. In it, he said he would get in touch. It would have been nice to be woken up with a kiss—or something even more passionate. But perhaps he hadn't wanted to disturb me. And truthfully, I could use the extra hour of sleep.

Dannie was dressed entirely in white today—smart white trousers, off-white leather trainers, and a relaxed-fit shirt with the top three buttons undone. The color suited him. Against the crisp, clean look of his outfit, his tan skin and tattoos stood out even more.

He didn't say much apart from the usual polite greetings—asking how I was and whether I'd slept well. Though he wasn't exactly grumpy, his energy wasn't as lighthearted as usual. Something was on his mind, that much was clear. But I didn't want to ask or get involved.

Mr. Huang, a friend of Dannie's, met us in the lobby and scanned us through the security barrier into the elevator section. His assistant, Amanda, handed each of us a visitor's card. I hung the blue lanyard around my neck.

Mr. Huang's office was on the twelfth floor. Apparently, his visa agency specialized in handling difficult cases—politicians, bloggers, journalists who had been denied entry for various reasons. His agency found ways to get them into China, provided they agreed not to cause trouble during their visit.

The agency occupied two floors. The eleventh floor was where the applications were processed, while the twelfth was strictly for staff and housed Mr. Huang's office.

After a quick tour, Mr. Huang excused himself, mentioning a meeting across town in Hong Kong.

Normally, Amanda would accompany him, but today, she had been assigned to personally handle my case.

We thanked Mr. Huang, and Dannie mumbled something about treating him to a meal and gifting his wife an exclusive, limited-edition luxury item. Then, when we were alone with Amanda, Dannie turned on his charm, promising to send her to Big-Her and let her pick out anything she fancied—his guy would handle the bill.

Amanda's demeanor shifted instantly. Gone was the polite, professional mask of someone merely doing her job. Suddenly, we were long-lost best friends. She led us to the cafe area, a space reserved for senior staff and government VIPs and served us drinks alongside an impressive selection of confections.

"Have you ever been to China before?" Amanda asked, clicking away on her laptop.

"No."

"Only Hong Kong?"

"Yes." I nodded.

"Do you have anyone who can vouch for you?"

"What do you mean?" I frowned in confusion. Dannie's hand rested lightly on mine.

He answered without hesitation. "I can."

"Thanks, Dannie. But I still don't understand the question. What exactly are you vouching for?"

"We need someone to confirm that you're a good character," Amanda explained. "A responsible citizen of..." She paused, glancing at my passport even though she had just filled out the nationality field. "The United States of America."

"My friend Wendy could do that. Should I give her a call?"

"She's American?"

"Yes."

"No, we don't—" Her gaze flicked between me and Dannie before settling back on me. "Your guarantor has to be a citizen of Hong Kong or the Republic of China and must have known you for at least five years."

"It's okay, June. I qualify." Dannie reassured me, giving Amanda a confirming glance.

"Yes, Mr. Wu is a perfect candidate," she affirmed.

"So, what does that mean? I still don't get it."

"Mrs. Wu—"

"Dr. Bennet," I corrected her before she could go any further.

"Oh... kay. Dr Bennet," she said, adjusting. "You don't intend to cause any trouble in China, do you?"

"What kind of trouble?" I asked warily. That wasn't my intention, of course, but I wasn't entirely sure what might be considered as "trouble" in some countries.

For example, while some categories of drugs were illegal in America, people weren't afraid of the legal repercussions that could come with the use of those drugs. But in many South East countries, the consequences could be far more severe. The thought of the death penalty sent a shiver through me.

Amanda let out a quiet sigh, clearly growing frustrated with my questions.

"Look, it's just a routine question we ask all our clients," she said. "Believe me, we pre-screen applicants before we even take them on. Your case is straightforward. You're a highly regarded doctor in the States. No debt. Not even a speeding ticket. Your application will go through without any issues. Normally, we'd send you straight to the visa center, so you wouldn't have to pay extra fees. But if it weren't for—"

Dannie cleared his throat. "I think June gets the idea now, right?" Then he turned to Amanda. "And I believe you have everything you need to process the application."

Amanda stood up and straightened her gray pantsuit —a smart, tailored short with a vest that I found both interesting and a little odd. It wasn't something I'd normally wear, but I could see myself trying something like that next summer.

Mr. Huang's assistant excused herself, murmuring, "be right back," before leaving us with our coffee.

The cafe had a steady flow of people coming and going, most of them in a hurry. They'd grab a takeaway cup from the barista and practically jog out the door. It couldn't be cheap to have a private barista serving only a select few, but maybe it saved time. Instead of employees running out to the city for their caffeine fix, the coffee came to them.

Then again, in this day and age, you could order anything with a few taps on your phone. Places like this didn't seem particularly sustainable in the long run.

"Are you worried about your visa?" Dannie broke through the chit chat in my head.

"Not after hearing what Amanda said," I admitted. Everything she had told me was correct. There was no reason my application should be rejected. And yet, a small part of me still worried they'd find something—

some trivial excuse to deny me entry. Maybe they'd dig up evidence of me watching porn online or something ridiculous like that.

"You don't have to sit with me," I told Dannie. "You must have a lot to do right?"

"Nothing important. It can wait."

I hesitated. Dannie was like that—always thoughtful in ways I didn't expect. "You didn't have to come at all."

"I had to be here anyway, as your guarantor." He replied, reminding me of that two second answer he'd given.

"Oh, right. That." I nodded, feeling bad that he was missing work, or whatever he did, because of me and that one silly question. "I didn't know about that part of the application process."

"I figured there might be something like that—kind of like when you apply for an American visa." He said, the words sliding of his tongue as he shrugged.

"What? I didn't know they had that requirement." I had never really thought about it from the other side, how easy or difficult was it for people to get a visa to the U.S.

"Yeah, but once you know the rules, it's fine. Just play along, give them what they want. At the end of the day, they're just doing their job. They want to keep their country safe." Dannie shrugged again, as if none of it really mattered.

"I suppose." I answered. He made sense. Dannie wasn't an unreasonable person. Sometimes I forget what he does for a living. TV and movies always painted people like him—mafias, triads, gangsters, whatever you wanted to call them—as violent, lawless men who took whatever they wanted. Maybe those movies were wrong. Or maybe I was just lucky with Dannie.

"What's your plan after this?" he asked.

"Get the first ticket to Shanghai." I let out a nervous chuckle.

"Okay. Let me know if you need help."

"I think I'll be okay."

We hadn't said anything to suggest this was a farewell, yet it felt like goodbye.

"I know a few people in Shanghai," Dannie continued. "Do you want me to arrange a place for you to stay?"

I hadn't thought much about accommodation. I just assumed Wendy and I would stay with Kai. Worst case scenario, we could always book a hotel. That was part of travelling, after all—figuring things out as we went.

"No, really. I think we'll be okay."

"Of course. Mr. Li will look after you." His voice carried a slight edge. Bitter.

I hesitated before asking, "By the way, why did you have the suite last night?"

I didn't think he had booked it for me and Kai to use. If he had expected to spend the night with me, I needed to know. I needed to clarify where we stood so he wouldn't get the wrong idea.

"It was reserved for me," he said simply.

"Really?" He had mentioned that before, but it still didn't make sense. "I can't believe a hotel would keep a suite reserved for you year-round. It doesn't seem very... economical."

"So, you think I booked it for another reason?"

"Maybe."

I took a sip of my latte for the first time. It was rich and bitter—real coffee. Not the weak, sugary kind I usually got from those green-logo chain stores.

Dannie leaned back in his chair. "You know I don't allow anyone into my apartment."

I did know that. He had told me before, but I hadn't fully processed what it meant.

"And it's necessary for me to keep the suite for..."

He trailed off.

He didn't need to finish his sentence. I suddenly realized what he meant.

He had needs. We all did. But he couldn't bring anyone back to his apartment. I understood that now.

I wasn't his wife—not really—but somehow, the way I questioned him made me feel like I was. And I couldn't help feeling a little embarrassed.

I was falling in love with Kai. As much as I hated to admit it, I knew it was true. But the thought of Dannie bringing women back to the suite still bothered me—like I had been given a toy, only to have it ripped from my hands forcibly, even though I had never owned it to begin with.

Fuck psychology.

Humans are complicated.

I should stop overanalyzing everything that crossed my mind.

"Got it. You don't need to explain yourself to me." Once I left Hong Kong, I might never see Dannie again. And I really should stay away from his business.

Amanda glided back into the cafe, the sharp click of

her red-bottom heels punctuating the quiet hum of conversation around us. I found myself wondering how much she made as an assistant. My gaze flickered to the latte in front of me—still warm, barely touched. I tapped my phone screen to check the time.

"Is everything okay?" Seeing her back so soon made me nervous. "Are you missing any information or something?"

"Oh no, everything is perfect. Here's your document. You can enter China freely for the next three years." Amanda handed me my passport along with a manila folder stuffed with supporting documents.

"Really? That was only..."

"Ten minutes. My personal best." She flashed a confident smile and threw a wink at Dannie.

"Thanks, Amanda. You're a star, as always."

"When will you visit again? I haven't seen you in, like... forever." Amanda flirted, her demeanor more relaxed now that Dannie seemed at ease. She pulled out a chair beside him and sat down.

"Your dad has been really busy, and I didn't want to intrude." Only then did I realize the connection between Amanda and Mr. Huang. She wasn't just any assistant— that explained her Instagram-famous aura and the luxury shoes she could somehow afford on an assistant's salary.

"Nonsense. We're always happy to see you. Dad's having a birthday party next month. You're coming, right?"

"Ah... yes. I'll be there."

I didn't remember seeing her last night. Maybe she wasn't there, or maybe I was too preoccupied to notice.

I thanked Amanda several times and promised her a tour of New York when she visited next. Meanwhile, Dannie made some vague arrangement to send her expensive gifts—though I was sure she and her father could afford them anyway. But then again, who turns down a free luxury gift?

"Should we grab something to eat?" Dannie's voice pulled me from my thoughts.

"I don't think so." My response came too quickly, too sharp, like I couldn't get away fast enough. "I'm sorry, but I need to get on the next available flight."

"Why don't we go back to my hotel? I'll have my secretary meet us there and book you and Wendy the next available flight. It'll be more efficient than handling everything on your phone."

He had a point. The last time I checked, Wendy got a room at the hotel, and we were supposed to finalize travel plans after I sorted out my visa.

"You're right." I squeezed out a smile, grateful to have a friend like Dannie who always had my best interests at heart.

Traffic in Hong Kong was chaotic in the morning, but with Dannie's driver waiting for us, we got back to the hotel with minimal hassle. I texted Wendy a couple of times but got no response.

Just as he promised, his secretary, whose name I couldn't remember—met us in the lobby. The three of us went to the hotel's breakfast buffet. A waiter immediately recognized Dannie and led us to a private corner, tucked behind a decorative screen near the floor-to-ceiling windows.

After taking our drink orders, the secretary peppered me with a few questions about my travel preferences—departure time, luggage allowance, seating choices—before setting up at a smaller table behind us to book the flights. My only request was the next available flight. Wendy and I didn't have much baggage, and I didn't care if I flew coach or business, aisle or window.

Dannie and I returned to our table with plates of food. His was a traditional Chinese breakfast—pickled vegetables and congee. Mine was a Western spread of a cheese omelet and toast.

"Western breakfast, huh?" Dannie mused, eyeing my plate.

"I tried to love congee, but it's really not my thing." I pushed a piece of toast through the yolk. "My mother swore by it as a cure-all. Whenever we were sick, she made us eat it with just a dash of soy sauce. My dad was the only one who escaped the forced feedings—being white gave him a pass. My brothers and I, though? We had no choice. Just looking at it gives me goosebump.

Dannie chuckled. "I don't love it either, but it's the best cure for a hangover."

"Oh... I didn't realize." I hesitated.

He had told me not to feel bad about being here this morning, but knowing he was dealing with a hangover changed things. "You shouldn't have come with me. I feel bad."

"I already told you—I wanted to." He slurped the rice porridge like it was best medicine.

I checked my phone again. Still no response from Wendy. Worried, I called her.

The moment she answered, I was met with irritated groans and half-mumbled curses. Apparently, I had interrupted a much-needed sleep—and an even more important dream featuring Mr. Bollywood. Grumpy and sleep-deprived, she refused breakfast and told me to update her once our flight was confirmed before promptly hanging up.

Dannie smirked. "Your friend is quite a character."

"I didn't think you noticed."

"I notice everything." He tapped my shoulder lightly, and our eyes met. His gaze held mine—steady, unreadable, intense.

"Dannie... I can't give you what you want."

We sat there, locked in silence, the weight of unspoken words pressing between us. The moment stretched unbearably until I forced myself to look away, overwhelmed by the awkwardness.

He swallowed hard, his Adam's apple bobbing. "I don't expect you to give me anything."

"Then stop being so nice to me." My voice wavered. "You make me feel—"

I couldn't finish the sentence. He made me feel a lot of things. His kindness was nothing but a burden, suffocating me.

"Feel what?"

"Bad. Guilty. Ashamed. Sad. I don't know... I'm not worth it."

"You're worth it."

Fuck.

That was the last thing I needed to hear.

I had literally just asked him to stop being nice.

My phone dinged. Grateful for the distraction, I grabbed it, my eyes scanning the screen as if my life depended on it.

My breath caught.

"Kai was taken by the police," I mumbled.

18

June

Wendy and I arrived at Shanghai International Airport about eight hours later. All flights from Hong Kong to Shanghai had been fully booked, but thanks to Dannie's assistant, we managed to secure seats.

The alternative was to charter a private plane, but that would have meant asking for another favor from my brother or Dannie. I could have reached out to Kai, but right now, he was with the police, and I didn't want to burden him with something as trivial as travel arrangements.

Wendy had shown up at the restaurant just five minutes after I heard about Kai. Her usual polished appearance was gone—no makeup, no perfectly styled hair—but she was ready to leave, her bags already packed. I didn't ask, but I assumed she must have heard the news herself from Trevon.

Dannie had dropped us off at the airport, and now we stood at the busy pickup point, waiting for Trevon.

"Are you sure we're in the right place?" Wendy asked, scanning the line of approaching cars.

"This is my first time here too, but I think so," I replied.

The area bustled with travelers like us, people who had just stepped off a plane, waiting to be picked up by taxis, private drivers, or loved ones.

Wendy fired off a series of questions—so many that it felt like thousands. I answered each one with nothing more than common sense, but part of me wondered why she was asking such obvious things. I was used to answering questions; it was second nature. Years of working with patients had trained me to encourage their curiosity, always reminding them—and myself—that there was no such thing as a stupid question.

But that wasn't entirely true. Some questions were, in fact, pointless.

"Why are there so many people here?"

"How much longer do you think we'll have to wait?"

"What kind of car does Trevon drive?"

"How did Trevon even get a car here?"

Honestly, how was I supposed to know? So, I gave her the best guesses I could.

"Maybe it's a holiday today."

"It won't be much longer."

"Something big enough to fit us both."

"He probably rented one."

As if on cue, a sleek white SUV pulled up in front of

us. The make was unfamiliar, but it looked expensive. The passenger door opened, and Trevon stepped out.

"How's Kai?" I asked eagerly. Trevon pulled me into a quick hug before doing the same with Wendy.

Before I could say more, a woman stepped out from behind him. I knew her face, but I couldn't immediately place her.

She extended a hand. "Andy."

I shook it. "June Bennet."

"I know. I worked in your office for two days."

"What?" My mouth dropped open. I couldn't believe I had never caught her name before. She was Kai's personal assistant, the one who had practically camped out in my reception area for two days. The same woman who had somehow charmed and befriended Siti, my receptionist-slash-assistant.

"I remember now."

"I don't think we've been properly introduced," she said.

"No, I don't think so." Embarrassment crept over me. This woman had worked under my roof for two days, and I hadn't even taken a moment to introduce myself.

"Andy drove me here," Trevon interjected, taking my small backpack and placing our minimal belongings into the trunk.

"Why don't you both get in?" Andy gestured toward the open car door. "I'll update you on everything you want to know about Mr. Li."

Wendy slid in first, and I followed. Andy shut the door behind us before getting into the driver's seat. Trevon took the passenger seat up front.

"Are you guys comfortable?" Andy asked, turning slightly to face us.

"Yes, you have a nice car," Wendy chimed in.

The interior was sleek and modern, with a distinct luxury feel. Functional, yet elegant.

"It's made in China," Andy explained. "Very cheap and affordable."

I nodded, though her comment made me wonder—was it as cheap as a second-hand car in the U.S.? Or was she joking? If she was, none of us were laughing.

"Are you taking us to Kai?" I asked, cutting to the point.

"No, Dr. Bennet."

"Call me June." I offered.

"If you insist."

"I do. Now, please—where is Kai?"

"Kai is with the police," Trevon answered.

"Are we going to the police station?"

"No, we won't be allowed in without permission." Andy pulled the car to a stop as traffic ahead stalled. "The police can't hold him much longer. As far as we know, he's only being questioned. He hasn't done anything wrong."

"Then what can we do? Does he have a lawyer?"

"Yes, Dr..." Andy cleared her throat. "June. Mr. Li's lawyer has been with him the whole time."

"What can we do?" My voice rose in frustration. "There has to be something we can do."

"June," Andy said patiently, "Mr. Li instructed me to take care of you. The only thing you can do right now is enjoy your time here in Shanghai."

"Enjoy myself?" I scoffed. "How can I enjoy myself knowing Kai is in jail?"

"Calm down, June." Wendy wrapped an arm around me in a reassuring squeeze.

I inhaled sharply, then exhaled—forcing myself to practice the same deep-breathing techniques I taught my patients. After a few seconds, I managed a steadier voice. "Okay, I'm sorry. I get it. Where are we going now?"

"We're heading to Mr. Li's apartment. He instructed me to take you both there."

I sighed, frustration still simmering beneath the surface. My questions weren't getting me anywhere. Either Andy wasn't willing to give me more information, or I wasn't in the right headspace to ask the right ones.

What I thought I wanted to know versus what was actually necessary blurred together in a tangled mess inside my head. My mind felt foggy, disorganized.

Maybe it was best to let someone with a clearer, calmer mindset take the lead.

"Andy, hi." My sudden greeting seemed to catch her off guard. "I think we got off on the wrong foot."

"What made you think that?"

A trembling smile spread across my face. "I must apologize for not recognizing you, for not properly introducing myself back in the States. I feel like a jerk. Really, for that alone, I'm truly sorry."

"Oh no, don't say that. Mr. Li, well, we were the ones in the wrong. We caused a lot of trouble for you and your patients. You were right to ignore us."

I suddenly missed Kai. I didn't know what he was doing at that moment, but I understood why he had tried to stay close to me. He was trying to protect me from Mack, afraid that Mack—or any of his accomplices—would show up and hurt me. After everything he had been through, there was no way he would ever willingly put himself at risk. Yet, he had. He knew what Mack was capable of, and he still chose to risk his safety to protect me.

A tear slipped down my cheek.

"Thank you. You're too kind. So kind that you didn't even notice how rude I was."

"Oh." Andy made a face, clearly uncomfortable with my sudden display of emotion.

"Can you tell me everything you know? How did you get involved in all this?"

The traffic was finally moving, though still at a crawl. I leaned forward slightly, straining to hear Andy over the hum of the city.

"After Ms. Law disappeared, I was asked to return to Shanghai and stand by for Mr. Li's arrival. As usual, I reported to our Shanghai office every day, just doing my job."

"Kai didn't contact you at all during that time?"

Andy honked at a motorbike that had suddenly swerved out from a side street, nearly causing an accident.

"These delivery drivers—so reckless." She rolled down the window and shouted something in Chinese. The rider yelled something back, unapologetic, before speeding away. With a sigh, she rolled the window back up.

"Sorry about that," she muttered. "No, Mr. Li didn't

contact me. But I didn't think twice about it. It's normal. Sometimes I don't hear from him for a week or two. Then, out of nowhere, he'll call me every fifteen minutes, throwing assignments at me left, right, and center."

"I see. Did he tell you to pick me up?"

The moment the question left my lips, I wanted to correct myself. What I had meant to ask was how she knew Kai wasn't in Shanghai, or how she had gotten in touch with Trevon. But I held back, wanting to see how she would respond.

"The police had been coming to the office," she said, her grip tightening on the wheel. "They couldn't reach him at his apartment or his parents' house. That's when I started getting worried. Then, as soon as I saw Mr. Li's booking for a private jet into Shanghai, I went to the airport to wait for him."

"And then?"

"Well, the police must have heard about it because they were pretty much waiting there with me. There was nothing I—or anyone—could do to stop them from entering the airport. When they took him—" Andy hesitated, her gaze flickering to my face for a brief moment. "Before Mr. Li went with them for questioning, he told me to look after Mr. Smith and make sure you had whatever you needed when you arrived."

"Have you heard from Kai since?"

"Not really. We haven't been given any information. But I can tell you this, Mr. Li has the best lawyer in the country. They'll do everything they can to help him. I'm sure of that."

"What about Jenny? Do you know anything about

her?" My words darted out of my mouth, pressing her for more information.

"No, I'm sorry."

"Is there anything you can do? Like asking her personal assistant or her bodyguard or something?"

I was certain that a good personal assistant had their own secret network. They somehow just knew every other assistant and could magically arrange for things to happen. Unless, of course, Kai had hired a pretty but clueless assistant—which was totally possible. For example, they always managed to book plane tickets for the desired dates, even last-minute ones. How they pulled it off still baffles me to this day.

But Andy was a woman in her mid-thirties, attractive in her own way, though not in a manner that would pique Kai's romantic interest. I had known Kai long enough to understand that Andy wasn't the type of woman he would take to bed. He had hired her for her qualifications and experience, not for her looks.

"Believe me, I tried to keep tabs on Ms. Law as soon as she went missing. But all information about her has been completely cut off. It's like no one is allowed to talk about it."

"Why do you think that is?"

"I don't know if I'm allowed to say this…"

"You can tell me anything." I didn't know how I knew, but something told me that she was hiding something. "I—we won't tell anyone that you told us this."

Trevon and Wendy both nodded in agreement.

"Usually, I can get any information from just about anyone. But this time, it's very different. I have a feeling they were specifically told to keep quiet—or else something bad might happen to them."

"Like what?"

"I don't know. When Ms. Law first returned, her personal assistant mentioned she wasn't in great shape. But the last time we spoke, she seemed scared—like she was afraid for her own safety just for telling me that. Then I asked about Ms. Law's family, her husband, but she refused to say anything."

"So that means some serious shit has gone down with that family, and they're trying to keep everyone's mouth shut." Wendy concluded.

She could be right. She was probably right. But I wanted to keep an open mind, to be a little more optimistic. Maybe the family was just very private.

"Where are we going now?"

"I'm taking you to Mr. Li's penthouse. You guys can stay there for the time being."

Then I remembered her saying that two minutes ago. My mind just hadn't caught up somehow. "Sorry, yes. You already said that."

A few minutes later, we arrived at Kai's apartment. Andy led us inside and handed us the door code. According to her, Kai had invested heavily in this building, ensuring the developers constructed it to his exact standards—modern, luxurious, and equipped with the latest security systems.

Andy gave us a quick tour of the apartment. It bore a striking resemblance to his place in New York, and I couldn't help but wonder which building had come first —and who had stolen the design from whom.

"That over there," she pointed to a sleek, glass-covered structure across from us, "is our Shanghai office, our Chinese headquarters."

I observed the building, idly wondering which floor Kai's office was situated on. It wasn't something I needed to know, but there was something oddly comforting about seeing people working behind the glass. Perhaps that was why he had chosen to live in the building across from it.

"That's very convenient, being so close to work."

"Yes," she replied matter-of-factly, then handed me a piece of paper. "Here's a list of numbers you can call for anything you might need. Dr. Liang is the building's doctor, and he's available 24/7 for medical issues—he can do house visits or send an ambulance if necessary. The fridge and pantry are stocked, but if you need anything else, you can call the housekeeping team. They'll be happy to assist."

"How do we get around?"

"I can drive you whenever possible."

"We can just call an Uber or something."

"We don't have Uber in China, but you can use Didi. It's pretty much the same thing. But honestly, you're Mr. Li's special guests from the United States, and I'm happy to help whenever possible."

"It's not your job to do that."

Wendy tapped my shoulder and gestured upstairs before disappearing with Trevon.

Andy paused.

"Yes and no. My job is to take care of Mr. Li's needs as best as I can. Right now, ensuring your well-being helps put his mind at ease while he deals with other matters." Her voice trailed off slightly at the end.

"Well then, thank you. Truth is, I don't know anyone here. It would be a huge help to have you around."

"My pleasure. Now, are you hungry? I can order food or cook."

"You can cook?"

Andy smiled. "Not well. But I can manage something simple like cup of noodles. Or I can get the chef up here."

"Chef?"

"Yes."

"Okay." I wanted to ask for more details, but my head was already spinning from all the information she had given me. "Will Kai come here when he finishes with the investigation?"

"That..." she hesitated. "This is Mr. Li's preferred place to stay."

"He has more than one home?"

Her gaze dipped before she looked back up. "Some nights, he stays at Mrs. Li's house. That is still his official address."

"Are you saying that he lives with his mother?" I laughed out loud. Despite the worries for him, I couldn't help but find the image of Kai, a well-known womanizer, living with his mother absolutely hilarious.

"Yes, it's our culture," Andy said flatly. "Unmarried people live with their parents unless they move away for work. Sometimes, even married couples live with their parents."

"I'm sorry for laughing. I actually knew that—my mother is half Chinese, and she tried to make me live with her," I said, still suppressing a chuckle. The thought of Kai, of all people, in such traditional setup was just too amusing. "So, this place is more like his bachelor pad?"

"I... I don't know what you mean."

I gave her a sideway glance, trying to gauge whether she was genuinely that naive or just pretending. As Kai's personal assistant, she had to be aware of his little obsession, his fondness for beautiful women. This had to be the place he brought them.

The doorbell rang and Andy hurried over to open it, letting in two young men who looked to be in their twenties. They greeted me politely before directing a few questions my way. After a brief discussion, we decided on traditional Shanghai home cooking.

While the cooks busied themselves in the kitchen, I sat at the dining table with Andy, who was clicking away on her laptop.

"What if I need help in the middle of the night and you're not here?" I asked, though I hoped it wouldn't come to that. Still, it was best to be prepared.

"You can call me," she replied without looking up.

"What if you don't pick up?"

Andy pulled off her glasses and placed them on the table.

"In that case, you can call the building reception. They have someone who speaks English, and they'll be able to assist you."

I nodded. So far, I'd been lucky with this trip—most of the people I'd encountered spoke decent English. "Do a lot of people speak English in Shanghai?"

"Depends on where you go," Andy said, her fingers

still poised over the keyboard. "You're fine in the city and the touristy areas. Are you planning to go somewhere? I can take you if you want."

"No." I shook my head. Sightseeing was the last thing on my mind while Kai was... I couldn't even bring myself to think the words.

Jail.

Police custody.

I forced the thought away. "I just need to know in case I have to handle something for Kai. You know..."

"I see."

Before either of us could say anything more, the sharp, urgent chime of the doorbell shattered the quiet. Andy froze, her brows furrowing.

"I... I don't know who that could be." Slowly, she got up from her seat. "The reception is supposed to call if we have a visitor."

19

Kai

The police weren't happy with my answers.

I didn't blame them. I wouldn't be either if I were in their shoes. They had the footage of Mario and me at the gate—aggressively breaking it down. They hadn't said it outright, but from what I gathered, I was their main suspect.

I had no idea why they kept repeating the same questions over and over, hoping I'd suddenly change my story. For a brief moment, I considered making something up just to mess with them. Ms. Zhang, my lawyer, shut that idea down fast. One wrong word, she warned, and I could ruin my life forever.

She also told me that Chen was still alive—barely. He was in the ICU, kept alive by machines, his life hanging by a thread. Jenny, however, wasn't able to cooperate with the police. When I pressed Zhang for details, she refused to answer while we were still at the station.

"Can you tell me what happened to my cousin now? Why are they letting me out? I haven't told them anything."

I sat inside Zhang's Volvo as her driver pulled away from the station. The car was far from luxurious, especially for someone like Zhang. She practically lived in the backseat, shuffling between meetings, yet the space barely fits her paperwork. When I'd asked for a ride, her driver had to relocate two bulky boxes from my seat to the trunk.

She hesitated. "I know you and Mrs. Chen. were close..."

That wasn't a good sign. If the news was minor, she would've told me by now.

"Just say it," I pressed. "Whatever you're hiding, it won't shock me."

Zhang sat up straighter, then cleared her throat. "She confessed—before they admitted her to the facility."

I froze.

"Wait." My voice rose as disbelief floored me. "What? What did she confess to?"

Zhang exhaled, barely audible. "She claimed she had been planning to kill her husband for a long time... and that you tried to stop her. But by the time you got there, it was too late."

"No." I shook my head, rejecting the words outright.

That wasn't true.

She loved that man.

She would never hurt him. Not on purpose.

"It was an accident," I insisted. "Why didn't you tell me this before? Is that why they let me out so fast?"

"Yes. The good news is—you're in the clear."

I swallowed hard, my chest tightening.

"I..." I struggled for breath, my mind spinning.

My poor cousin.

"What facility is she in?" My fingers instinctively tugged at my already loosened tie. It felt like my lungs couldn't find enough air.

"The psychiatric hospital in Shanghai," Zhang answered. "When they found her, she couldn't speak. Couldn't move. It was as if she had completely shut down. Like..."

"Like what?" My voice was barely a whisper.

"Like a sack of rice," she said flatly. "Floppy. Just lying there, unable to do anything."

It didn't make sense.

If she was really unresponsive when they found her—how the hell did she confess?

Something wasn't adding up.

"Is it possible someone made that up? That she never actually confessed?"

Zhang studied me. "What makes you say that?"

"Because—," I paused, dark memories flooded back, thick with guilt. "She was quite out of it when I left her."

The hours in that tiny interrogation room had been a slow, grinding torture. The officers took turns hammering me with the same questions, over and over, hoping exhaustion would break me.

If I'd heard about Jenny's so-called confession then—if I'd known she had relapsed and been locked up—I might have cracked. I might have confessed to something myself. Lied. Said whatever they wanted to hear.

Just to save her.

"Is she any better now?"

Zhang exhaled. "No one really knows. The only reason I even found out was because I went to the house and spoke with the housekeeper. She wouldn't say anything at first, but when she realized I represented you, she finally told me."

I nodded, appreciating the housekeeper's loyalty to Jenny. She had always looked out for her, stepping in whenever things got bad. There were times she had even called me, pleading for help—begging me to come and get Jenny or at least do something to ease the situation.

"Is she one of yours?" Zhang asked, frowning before shooting me a pointed look.

"No. She's just a kind woman." The words didn't sound convincing, even to me. Truth was, I had never considered planting someone at Chen's house. If I had, things wouldn't have spiraled out of control the way they did. I wouldn't have been left scrambling to pick up the pieces after it was too late.

"Believe it or not, I never even met her—until that day." The realization unsettled me. I couldn't believe I had never made the effort to meet or even acquaint myself with the woman who had been quietly helping Jenny all this time.

"Anyway," Zhang said, shifting the subject, "try not to leave the country in the meantime."

I rolled my eyes at the way she said *try*. She hadn't asked me a single question about what really happened that day. Not once. It was clear—whether I was involved or not, she didn't care.

My life was now deeply entangled with Chen's fate. If he died, the case would almost certainly be ruled as murder.

If he lived, we would be at his mercy. He could dismiss everything, call it an accident, a suicide attempt, whatever we eventually settled on. Or he could press charges for attempted murder.

"Thanks for everything," I said politely, signaling for the driver to drop me off by the roadside.

I waved as Zhang's car drove away.

Two seconds later, I slipped into one of my black SUVs, following right behind Zhang's car.

"Tell me everything you know."

I didn't bother greeting Clare.

"Yes boss," she said, which was about as warm a welcome as I was going to get today. She dove straight into the details, recounting everything she had uncovered.

I was irritated to find that she hadn't gathered much more than what my lawyer had already told me.

"Mario is in hiding."

Finally. I nodded slightly, satisfied. When the time comes, he could be a key witness. For now, I was just relieved he was staying out of the spotlight—Mario and authority figures didn't mix well.

"And there's news about Dave."

My chest tightened. "Where is he? Is he okay?"

Clare nodded.

That was the best news I'd heard all day. If I could, I'd go find him myself. Dave had practically raised me—he was the one who looked after me when my parents couldn't. Ever since the kidnapping, he hadn't left my side. Until now.

Clare's eyes shimmered with emotion. "He's okay. He's in private care, under Dr. Bennet's medical team."

"Dr. Bennet? How?"

"Oh— not Dr. June Bennet." She tapped her lips like she could erase the slip. "I meant her brother, Liam Bennet. Our team found Dave abandoned in a rental car registered to Mack just outside of New York. Mr. Young had him sent to his brother for treatment."

"Good man," I muttered.

That was Lincoln—always there when I needed him.

"Yes, Mr. Young had been a great help. His source got us the information we needed to find Dave."

"Wait, Mack isn't that stupid—he wouldn't just leave Dave in a car registered to his name. He knew we were looking for Dave. He left us a trail on purpose."

Clare frowned. "Huh. I hadn't thought of that. I figured we just got lucky."

Maybe. It would've been nice to believe that luck was on our side. But Mack had been working for Dannie for years. Dannie was no fool—he wouldn't keep an idiot around for nothing.

"What did Liam say?"

Her expression darkened. "It's bad. They beat him up. He took a gunshot to the thigh, lost a lot of blood— nearly died. Luckily, Mr. Young's team found him. If they hadn't, the police might have gotten involved."

My nerves rattled at the mention of the word gun.

I closed my eyes.

Deep breath one.

Deep breath two.

Deep breath three.

"Is his life still in danger?"

"No."

"That's all I need to know for now."

If Liam wasn't the one looking after Dave, I would have personally sent in a team of medical experts no matter the cost.

I hated feeling helpless when it came to protecting the people I cared about.

"Okay," I muttered to myself. We had found Dave, and he was alive. That was one massive weight off my shoulders.

Chen being alive, that was a miracle. The image of him covered in blood was still fresh in my mind, like it had happened just minutes ago. I had been convinced he wasn't breathing. And as much of an asshole as he was, I could never wish death upon anyone. Not even him.

Jenny.

There wasn't much I could do for her right now. She had been in a facility before when things got bad. At least for now, no one could harm her.

"I want to be the first to hear about cousin Jenny. See what you can do."

"Noted, boss. I know someone." Clare offered a faint smile, her confidence seeming to recover.

"June? She has to be here by now."

Unless Dannie had found some dumb excuse to keep her. Or chained her down and forced her to have his baby. A sudden heat surged through my spine at the thought.

"Dr. Bennet, Ms. Gupta and Mr. Smith are all here. Andy said she'd look after them."

"Where are they now?"

"They should be at the penthouse."

"Take me there." I demanded.

"Actually, are you sure you don't want to go home first?"

I didn't like Clare's tone. This was exactly what irritated me about her. Now that her confidence was back, she thought she could boss me around. And it was my fault—I had let her get away with this behavior for far too long. Her demanding nature had been amusing at first, but I should have put an end to it the moment it started to annoy me.

"I'm going home."

"No, I mean to Mrs. Li."

"I don't want to go to my mother's house." I spat out the words. I knew exactly what she meant the first time. There was a reason I had bought my own apartment in Shanghai. My mother would have objected to the idea of me living on my own. As a traditional Chinese mother, she would never want her only son to move out. Maybe things would be different if she weren't the way she was. Sometimes, I just needed space.

A little distance.

A little air.

"Noted." Clare said with a curt nod and she looked away, sensing my annoyance, no doubt.

Finally.

Uncle He, my driver for many years, had already taken the initiative, steering us toward my apartment. Clare didn't know that. She was terrible with directions—she could never tell north from south, east from west.

No one spoke on the way there. Yet my mind felt unbearably loud. Scenes from the recent past collided with imagined futures. What was going to happen?

To me?

To Jenny?

To Chen?

When we finally arrived at my building, I exhaled in relief. My driver dropped me off by the elevator in the basement parking lot. I fidgeted, hands trembling slightly as I waited for the lift to carry me up.

Coming home felt... strange. The ride to the penthouse seemed almost unfamiliar, as if I were returning for the first time.

I stood at my own door and rang the bell.

Clare reached for the number pad, probably thinking I had forgotten the code. I pushed her hand away.

Waited.

Then the door opened.

There she was.

June.

It was actually Andy who opened the door, but June was the one who ran toward me, throwing her arms around my neck.

My world stopped.

The noise faded.

The headache that had been hammering in my skull disappeared.

I could have stayed like that forever—holding her, feeling her warmth—if she hadn't pulled away.

"Is everything okay, Mr. Li?" Andy asked in English. I suspected it was for June's benefit

I rubbed June's shoulder lightly before turning to Andy. "Thank you for taking care of things while I was gone. Have you been home since...?"

"Briefly."

I understood what she meant. When I found out about her divorce, I tripled her salary. Being a single mother in Shanghai wasn't easy.

"You should go home to your kid."

"It's not a problem, Mr. Li."

Andy could now afford a live-in au pair to care for her child because of the raise. Knowing I had a loyal employee I could count on in times of need made me smile.

"Honestly, I'm okay. Go home."

"I will. I'm just..." I squinted at her as she turned away, "...just need to quickly check through everything. Make sure everything is in order."

June kissed me on the cheek. Then my nose. Then my lips.

"Are you okay?" she asked.

"I am now."

I had been scared out of my mind when they took me. But I hid it well—or at least I liked to think I did.

The only thing that had kept me steady, the mantra I

had repeated in my head over and over, was simple: *Make June proud.*

Every time the police questioned me, I asked myself— would my answer make June proud? Even when exhaustion tempted me to say something reckless, to crack a stupid joke just to relieve the tension, I forced myself to stay in control.

It didn't always work.

People knew they shouldn't do stupid shit under stress, but they still did it. It was human nature.

But I was home now. With her.

I scooped June into my arms, ready to take her to my bedroom.

A sudden, urgent knock on the door stopped me.

June tensed in my arms. "Did you leave anyone behind?"

"It can't be Clare, right? I thought she came in." I tried to recall, but my attention had been on June—and briefly on thanking Andy for looking after her.

I stood frozen in the doorway, still holding June. I wanted to open the door, but I didn't want to put her down.

"I got it."

Andy moved past me and pulled the door open.

"Biaozi."

Bitch.

I stared in shock. My mother's voice. Her words.

"Mama?"

She practically stormed inside the room, her face twisted with fury. Before I could react, she grabbed June by the hair and wrenched her out of my arms.

Lucy followed close behind, tears streaming down her face.

June shoved my mother off. My mother retaliated, shoving back—once, twice—until June lost her balance and fell hard onto the floor.

Without thinking, I rushed to her side, reaching for her.

"Why wouldn't you help your own mother?" My mother shrieked in Shanghainese.

The last time I checked, she was still standing. June was the one on the ground. Had karma finally made my mother lose her footing?

Lucy hurried to help my mother.

"You gave up a girl like Lucy for an American whore like her?"

My head spun. What the hell was happening?

"What's going on?" June clung to me, her voice shaken.

"You're a whore." My mother lunged again, reaching past me. I did everything I could to shield June, but my mother still managed to strike her.

With one hand, I grabbed hold of my mother's shoulder while turning to check on June. Tears streaked her face. Her left hand clutched her cheek—red, angry, burning.

The room had filled.

Wendy. Trevon. Clare. All watching.

"Clare, hold my mother down."

"But, sir..." Clare hesitated. I knew she saw my mother as her real boss.

"Do it or get the fuck out."

Thankfully, she obeyed without further protest.

I exhaled sharply, switching to English. "Calm down, Mother."

I knew full well my Oxford-educated mother understood every word.

June still hadn't spoken.

"What the fuck is going on?" Wendy demanded, stepping beside June and gripping her arm protectively.

"This woman," my mother spat, "she's the reason for everything."

"For what?" Wendy's voice sharpened, her hand now planted firmly on her hip.

"Son, I know you wouldn't have gotten into trouble if it weren't for her." My mother's voice cracked as she jabbed a perfectly manicured finger at June.

I stepped between them, blocking her line of fire. "Mama, your son gets into trouble with or without her."

She knew that. She had to.

I was sure she had seen the financial statements—she must have noticed the absurd security expenses, the money I spent on my so-called entertainment—but she had never said a word.

"And Jenny," she continued, her voice trembling. "Poor Jenny would never have done anything so reckless if she hadn't been exposed to her American ways."

"Jenny only met her a few days ago," I shot back.

"Exactly! You see?" My mother's eyes flashed, as if she'd proven some grand point.

"Auntie," Lucy interjected timidly, stepping closer. "June did nothing but help us."

My mother softened—only slightly—as she turned to

Lucy. "Don't worry, sweetie. I already see you as my daughter-in-law. No one can take that away from you."

"What are you talking about?" I asked, my patience wearing thin.

"Clearly, you need a good woman by your side. And you're going to marry Lucy."

"No."

"Oh, you will."

My mother turned away from me and flicked her wrist at June, as if dismissing her. "Oi, you—how much do you want?"

June blinked. "What?"

"How much money do you want?"

"What the hell are you doing?" I demanded, glaring at my mother. She's lost her mind, that's the only explanation I could think of.

"Son, just like all those women you dated before, she only wants your money. *Our* money."

"What are you talking about?" My voice was tight, vibrating with anger. I hated her in this moment—this arrogance, this belief that she was above everyone, that everything had a price tag.

"Oh, come on," she scoffed. "Those women you dated back in college—why do you think none of them stuck around?"

A sinking feeling formed in my gut. "What have you done?"

"I paid them off."

"You did *what*?"

She rolled her eyes, it was nothing more than a mild

inconvenience. "Relax. Not all of them, of course. Only the *unsuitable* ones."

She turned back to June, dismissive, calculating. "Half a million. Is that enough?"

"Fuck, you're bleeding, June." Wendy's low voice cut through the chaos.

My headache roared back. My ears were ringing.

20

———

June

"Where?"

I hadn't felt anything. From Wendy's reaction, I knew it couldn't be that serious, otherwise, she would have been screaming at the top of her lungs.

Everyone was staring at me. Suddenly, I felt like I was trapped in one of my nightmares—standing in the middle of the school hall in my pajamas, wearing the wrong shoes, as everyone turned to laugh.

I braced myself, convinced the laughter was about to begin.

"Look what you did," Kai said, his sharp gaze piercing through his mother.

She folded her arms across her chest, completely unapologetic. "That whore deserved it."

Never in my life had I been called a whore. And I had no idea what I had done to deserve the title.

I touched my face, glancing down at my fingers. Blood. Not much, but enough. It stung when I pressed.

"I'm okay," I muttered lamely.

I hated confrontations. And Kai's mother had come here prepared for one. My gut told me she wouldn't leave without getting what she came for. Sooner or later, I would have to meet her halfway. But right now, I didn't have the energy to deal with her.

Tears had been streaming down Lucy's face since the moment she stepped inside. Judging by her smeared makeup, they had started long before she got here. I had so many questions for her, and I was sure Kai did too. She had disappeared with Jenny—and now, after all this time, she was suddenly here.

She owed us an explanation.

Kai's mother pulled a card from her white, diamond-studded Birkin bag and held it out. "Here. There's one million dollars in this card. Take it and leave."

She flicked the card across the room like some kind of magician performing a card trick.

"What the fuck are you doing? And how the hell did you even get into the building?" Kai's voice was sharp, laced with frustration.

Mrs. Li ignored his questions, pacing around him in her flawless white suit—probably couture. Her heels clicked softly against the floor as she tipped forward on her toes, scrutinizing him.

"Can't you see what this whore is doing to you?" she spat "Not only are you raising your voice to me, but you're also swearing at me—over her. Do you not see how this woman has poisoned your mind?"

Kai scoffed. "Mother, I've had enough of you controlling my life. I respect you for raising me, for doing it alone, but you don't get to dictate who I date."

Wendy nudged me and pressed a small box into my hands, marked with a red cross.

"Do you need help?" Kai's voice softened as he turned to me, concern flickering in his eyes. It was like he had a switch—loud one second, tender the next. The shift was seamless, effortless.

I shook my head and silently followed Wendy into the kitchen.

I splashed cool water onto my face at the sink, relieved to finally have a moment of peace. But when I turned around, the entire party had followed me, scattered throughout the space.

"If anything happens to her face—"

"So what?" Mrs. Li cut in before anyone could finish. "She can pay for plastic surgery herself with the money I'm giving her. Hell, I'll give her another million. Money is not an issue."

She waved a dismissive hand, her voice dripping with disdain.

For a fleeting moment, when she had finally let me walk away from that hallway, I thought maybe she had softened. Maybe she felt guilty for clawing into my skin with her needle-sharp nails.

But no.

Maybe not.

"I'm not taking your money," I said, dabbing disinfectant along the scratch, using my phone's selfie camera as a mirror.

"You all say that," Mrs. Li scoffed. "But nobody says no to money."

Kai's jaw clenched.

"Who exactly have you paid off, Mother?" His voice was low, controlled—but the red creeping up his neck said otherwise.

"You don't need to know."

"Tell me," he demanded, slamming his palm onto the dark marble countertop. "Or after today, you won't have a son anymore."

Mrs. Li barely flinched.

"I don't have the full list memorized," she said with an exaggerated sigh. "Most of your little college girlfriends. The whores from your filthy hobby."

She wrinkled her nose in disgust. "Honestly, son, you never know what kind of diseases those women carried."

Kai stiffened. "You knew?"

It could only mean one thing—his secret obsession with the darker world of sex.

"I know everything," she said smoothly. "Like father, like son. If I had agreed to—"

"Shut the fuck up, Mama." Kai's hands flew up in front of her mouth as if he could physically stop the words from spilling out.

She smirked, unfazed. "Come on. You know I did this for your own good."

That line.

The one parents always used to guilt trip their children into submission. A mind game played so often it worked like magic—until the magic wore off.

"No," Kai said, his voice razor-sharp. "You did this for you."

I set the disinfectant aside, deciding to leave the wound uncovered. It wasn't deep enough to need a dressing. Still, as I listened to their exchange, I silently calculated the best moment to slip out of the room.

"People like us don't marry for love. You know that."

"We marry for power, right? Or is it for more money? Money we couldn't possibly spend in a lifetime—hell, not even if our future generations lived like undead vampires? Look at you and Dad. Do you honestly want me to end up like you?"

I brushed my fingers lightly over Wendy's hand, catching her attention with a subtle tilt of my head toward the door. She dropped her chin in understanding.

Moving as if I were stepping on rice paper—something I'd picked up from my brief, and frankly unimpressive, Aikido training—I crept toward the exit. This wasn't about a sneak attack. I just needed to get out of there unnoticed.

Kai was too busy ripping apart his mother's ideology, pointing out the disaster that was her marriage, how his father had walked away and found real love. Proof, according to him, that everyone needed love.

I almost made it.

Smack.

A sharp sting radiated from my fresh wound. But this time, her hand wasn't on me.

It was on Kai.

"I'll marry June," he declared, his palm pressing against his reddened cheek.

It wasn't a proposal. It was a statement. A challenge. Unromantic.

"You will not," Mrs. Li and I protested at the same time.

Well, that was unexpected. Seemed like we finally had something in common.

"Why not?" Kai countered. "She's perfect. Exactly how I imagined my wife would look."

Still, it didn't sound like love. Not even close.

A nervous chuckle slipped my lips, thin and forced.

Was that all anyone ever saw in me? The perfect wife?

Dannie had certainly thought so years ago.

"*Lucy* is the perfect wife. Beautiful. Smart. From a prestigious family." Then Mrs. Li threw me a withering look. "Chinese, through and through."

Ouch.

I had never truly faced racism until now. And I couldn't believe it was coming from my own people.

Lucy had stopped crying. Yet, she hadn't said a word to defend herself. How could she just stand there and let Mrs. Li talk about her like that? Like she was some kind of prized possession on display. Unless... she wanted to marry Kai.

"Will you marry me June?"

"Kai..."

Before I could even say no, a sharp pain sliced through me. I gasped and looked down.

Mrs. Li's hand was clenched into a fist, gripping something.

A nail file.

I was bleeding. Again.

The stab couldn't have been deep. Whatever expensive nail file rich people bought, it couldn't be *that* sharp—could it? My mind scrambled for logic as I forced myself to breathe.

In. Out. In. Out.

I wasn't going to bleed out. I was going to live. That much was clear.

Breathe. Focus on nothing but breathing.

Then I was yanked backward. A collective gasp erupted in the room. Faces twisted in alarm, concern, helplessness.

No, I hadn't just fallen.

Mrs. Li had grabbed a handful of my hair and pulled. Hard.

I barely managed to catch myself before I hit the ground. If I hadn't, I would have lost a good chuck of my hair along with my dignity.

"Careful what you say next," she hissed.

The not-so-pathetic nail file was now pressed against my neck.

"What the fuck are you doing, Mama."

"Language, Kai."

"Mommy," he pleaded, his voice suddenly small. "Please, let her go."

"Wait for it…" Her laughter cracked through the air, shrill and piercing, sending a chill down my spine.

"Say it," she sneered, yanking my hair like I was nothing more than a ragdoll. "Say you're not going to marry him."

"No, of course not," I gasped. "We've only been on, what—one or two dates?"

"You hear that, son?" Another laugh, sharp and mocking. "And yet, you already fucked this whore, didn't you? What more do you want? Haven't you had your fill?"

"Let her go," Wendy demanded.

"Shut up." Mrs. Li spat. "You're exactly the same. Just like her. Denying your own roots. Calling yourselves American. Prancing around town like you're open for anyone to fuck you."

"Stop insulting her," Kai growled, his voice edged with barely contained rage. "You don't know the half of it."

"We're the worst. I admit it. My mother used to say the same thing about me." I said, hoping to appease the crazy woman.

Mrs. Li had lost control of her emotions. If I had to guess—judging by her erratic mood swings and what Kai said earlier—she suffered from some kind of mental disorder. There was no official diagnosis, but I knew one thing for certain: we had to try a different approach.

"You hear that?" Her hand jerked, and the dull edge of her nail file sawed against my throat. I leaned back, trying to ease the pressure.

"What else did she say?" she demanded.

"Oh, a lot actually." I forced out a laugh, though my heart pounded against my ribs. "I can tell you all about it over coffee."

"Yes, Ma. June's not that bad." Kai's voice was surprisingly steady. "Her mother is half-Chinese. She's actually here in China to learn more about her roots."

I had no idea what he was thinking. Mrs. Li had been keeping tabs on Kai—his whereabouts, his life, the women he had been seeing. She must have known why I was here.

"No." She tightened her grip on my hair, yanking my head back once more. "I don't want to ever see her in your life. I want her gone. Now."

"Of course, I'll take that million-dollar offer." I swallowed hard, trying to ignore the sharp sting on my scalp. "I don't even like Kai that much."

"That hurts," Kai muttered, playing along with my game like he could read my mind.

"You think I'm stupid?" she snapped, "What made you change your mind so quickly?"

She struck me on the head with the back of the nail file. The impact rattled through my skull, but I didn't dare react. I thought about running, but the moment I even considered it, she pressed the file against my throat again.

"Do you know how long I've known Kai?" I asked carefully.

"Yes. What are you getting at?"

"I had a crush on him when I was eighteen."

"He was a dreamboat back then..." she mused, her laugh softer this time, almost nostalgic.

"Yes. Perfect. Still is. But, you know, we American girls prefer American boys." I wasn't sure if this was the best angle, but playing the American card might be my only way out with a racist like her. "Falling for Kai wasn't an option, so I did what I knew best."

"And what is that?"

"Fucked him out of my system."

She let out a sharp, hysterical laugh, throwing her head back.

"See, I was right. She's a whore."

"I didn't want to admit it, but yes, you're right." The words stung, even though I didn't mean what I was saying. I could only pray my subconscious didn't start believing them.

"Look, baby," she turned to Kai. "I'm the only person in this world who truly cares about you. All these women... they come and go."

"Can I go now?" I asked, testing my luck. Her grip on my hair had relaxed, and the madness in her laughter had faded slightly.

"Not yet."

"I promise I won't see him again." I could tell she was close to letting me go. She just needed a little more convincing. "I'm actually married, you know? To someone really powerful. In Hong Kong."

Her eyes narrowed. "Oh? Is that true?"

"Yes, Dannie Wu. Have you heard of him?" Wendy, bless her, jumped in. "Triad. Boss of a triad."

Mrs. Li scoffed. "No way. This little mouse? What did he see in her?"

I couldn't help but feel a little offended. Okay, more offended than I already was. I took a deep breath and said, "he's a very angry man. If he finds out what happened here... he'll want some sort of payback."

"Bullshit."

"No, no bullshit." Wendy pulled out her phone, and suddenly, Dannie's voice rang out over the speaker.

Fuck.

This was getting out of hand.

"Hey Dannie," Wendy said, her voice calm. "We're in

a bit of a situation here. Can you tell Kai's mother that June is your wife?"

"What's going on?" Dannie's voice was sharp. "Put me on video."

"No—" I started, but it was too late. His face appeared on the screen.

"Dannie," I whispered.

"June."

A brief pause. Then his voice turned cold.

"Let her go, Auntie Yan. Or you'll be burying your son tomorrow."

Mrs. Li let out a short chuckle. "Oh, it's you, Dannie boy. Long time no see."

The ache in my scalp disappeared as she finally released her grip on my hair. My stomach lurched, but I remained still.

Everyone in the room exchanged nervous glances, but no one moved. No one dared to act.

What the hell have I gotten myself into?

"What do you want, Auntie Yan?" Dannie's voice was casual, but there was steel beneath it. "I can give you anything. You know I can. You just need to let my wife go."

"How could you, Dannie?" she scoffed. "How could you let your wife seduce my son like that? I know men like you sleep around, but how could you let your woman do the same? Aren't you embarrassed?"

Dannie let out a deep, amused chuckle. "Don't be ridiculous, Auntie. We live in a modern world. If I get to sleep around, she should be allowed to do the same.

That's the secret to a happy marriage. Equal rights and all, remember?"

Mrs. Li's laughter rang through the room, this time almost giddy. "Ah, I see, I see. You young people and your open marriages."

"You get it," Dannie agreed smoothly.

"But what do you think your parents would say if they were here?"

Dannie's expression darkened instantly. He hated anyone bringing up his deceased parents. Mrs. Li must have known them.

"Auntie Yan," he cut in, "let's end this. I know this isn't really you, and I won't let one of your episodes harm my woman."

Mrs. Li hesitated, but then she sighed. "But can you keep an eye on her?"

"Of course. I didn't know she was messing with the wrong boy, that's all."

"Okay." She giggled.

I could barely believe it. She was letting me go.

Though I hadn't been able to study her face closely, her laughter, her behavior—her wild mood swings—confirmed what I already suspected. She had been like this for a while. And it didn't seem like she was receiving any kind of treatment.

Whatever she had, it could be genetic. The same thing Jenny had. God, I hope I'm wrong.

As soon as she released me, my legs moved on their own. My head told me to keep my mouth shut, to not provoke her. But instead of walking away, I staggered toward Kai.

I threw myself at him.

Only for him to dodge to the side.

Trevon caught me before I hit the ground, saving me from further humiliation. It was probably for the best. At least I hadn't landed flat on my face.

Next thing I knew, Kai had rushed to his mother's side, speaking in a tone I had never heard from him before—gentle, patient, almost like a father soothing his beloved child.

Tears burned down my cheeks, hot and urgent.

Wendy appeared beside me, gripping my arm where Trevon wasn't. Her voice was barely a whisper, cautious not to disturb the fragile calm that had settled. "We should leave now."

I swallowed hard and nodded. "Let's go."

"Do you want to stay with Kai?" she asked Trevon, though I knew it was a loaded question. "I think it's best you stay with him."

Maybe I was overanalyzing, but Wendy had always been two steps ahead. We didn't always agree on her methods, yet somehow, she had saved me time and time again.

"Thank you for calling Dannie." My voice was hoarse. I had no idea when or how she got his number, or if I should feel betrayed that she had gone behind my back to befriend him.

"No problem," she said simply.

"He asked me to look out for you." She explained, then added, "Kai couldn't help you, so I thought I'd try him."

She was right.

To be fair to Kai, he had tried.

He just... failed.

And in my book, effort counted for something. But still, the realization clawed at me—the man I was falling hopelessly in love with hadn't been able to save me.

Love wasn't black and white.

Even when people cheated, I always tried to see the other side, to find the reason, the justification. Maybe they were actually meant to be. Like King Charles III of the United Kingdom and his one true love.

I gritted my teeth as I limped toward the exit, pressing a hand to my stomach. Blood still oozed from the wound. The vicious woman had stabbed me hard—with a blunt knife, no less.

And God, it hurt so much worse than a clean cut.

Just as I reached the door, I heard it.

Loud and clear.

"I will marry Lucy."

ALSO BY

Also by Summer Cooper

DARK DESIRES
A billionaire dark romance series
Dark Desire
Dark Rules
Dark Secret
Dark Time
Dark Truth

BARRE TO BAR
A billionaire second chance series
Dancing With Lies
Dancing With Temptation
Dancing With Doubt
Dancing With Guilt
Dancing With Redemption

TWISTED INTENTION

A billionaire revenge romance series
Twisted Beauty
Twisted Love
Twisted Fate

Mafia's Obsession
A hot mafia romance series
Mafia's Dirty Secret
Mafia's Fake Bride
Mafia's Final Play

Screaming Demons
An MC romance series full of suspense
Rough Start
Rough Ride
Rough Choice
Rough Return
Rough Patch
Rough Road
Rough Trip
Rough Night
Rough Love
Check out Summer's entire collection at
www.summercooper.com/books

Also by Susu Chin
Billionaire's Promise

ABOUT THE AUTHORS

About Summer Cooper

Besides (obviously!) reading and writing, she also loves cuddling her dogs, shouting at Alexa, being upside down (aka Yoga) and driving her family cray-cray!

Follow Summer on Facebook | Instagram| Goodreads | Bookbub

Get in touch at
hello@summercooper.com

www.summercooper.com

About Susu Chin

Susu Chin is a passionate romance writer making her debut Billionaire's Promise co-writing with Summer.

She's already at work on her next project, promising even more heart-racing and swoon-worthy moments for her readers.